The Deceitful Woman

M.L. Lexi

Copyright

To mothers.

Copyright

To mothers.

Everyone is hiding something—always.

—M.L. Lexi

Prologue

IT WAS TWO a.m.

Things were quiet. There was no sound in the room or outside. But for the sliver of hallway light that shimmered through the half-closed door, the room was dark.

Madison was exhausted from what she had endured the past six hours and fast asleep. The powder-blue hospital bedcover raised to her chest warmed her anemic body. Her makeup had washed off, and her face looked sallow and haggard. Her long, black hair was a knotted mess around her young, heart-shaped face.

Madison looked awful but peaceful in sleep.

It was now five a.m.

Someone had closed the door and rolled down the window blinds. The room was pitch dark.

Madison thought she heard footsteps from somewhere in the darkened room, maybe one person, possibly two people. She heard a voice, a soft murmur, perhaps that of a man and a woman. Two women?

"Who's there?" Madison's voice was slurred, incoherent, and barely audible.

Madison thought she heard a cry. Yes, it was a baby's cry. Maybe. Madison wasn't sure. Her head was swimming in confusion.

Where was she? Madison tried hard to remember.

Nothing came to her. She was too dazed, her mind too clouded. They must have given her drugs, something strong for the pain to calm her nerves.

Madison thought she saw a flash of light for a few seconds. She thought she heard wheels rolling on the tiled floor. There was a creaking sound. What creaked? Her mind was too fuzzy to form coherent thoughts, her vision too blurry to paint images.

Voices, one, two, possibly three, said something. A vague murmur. Madison thought she heard uncertainty and panic in one of the voices and confidence in the second.

The first voice said, "Relax, I've got this. It's all right." Maybe. The voice sounded familiar.

Whose voice was it? Madison tried to reach into her memory, but she came up blank.

"Who are you?" Madison's soft voice was hoarse, bristling with fear.

A hush followed, and the silence came and stretched.

Through her squinting eyes, Madison made out the vague movement of shadows. There was the smell of something flowery. No, it smelled of creamy sandalwood or musk with a touch of lavender, Madison determined after a few seconds. It was a comforting scent with familiar notes.

She couldn't figure out what was happening around her, but instinct clenched her insides and tightened her chest.

Madison warred with her mind to snap clear, but the darkness came now.

Part I

The Beginning

Secrets are the universal language of survival.

—M.L. Lexi

Chapter 1

Five Years Later

THE AIR WAS ripe with the scent of coffee and the sound of grinding beans. A commercial for a dream Caribbean destination lashed from the television screen that hung between the menu boards. Despacito flowed from the overhead speakers. Those waiting to place their order bobbed their heads to its picante rhythm. The tables and the bench seats were crowded with the after-school crowd of voluble teenagers in hoodies, jeans, and white trainers ingesting more caffeine than needed.

Lacy leaned a hip against the counter and stared at her daughter. "Organic milk only, Maddie," Lacy said and watched Madison on the opposite side of the counter set down the carton of skim milk in her hand and reach into the refrigerator for the organic milk.

Madison waved the carton of milk at her mother. "Satisfied?" she said after pouring into the tall coffee cup.

Nodding, Lacy flicked her eyes to the cold-cut sandwich in the display case. "And how about one of those subs, heated, to go?

"It's a Panino, not a sub." Madison snapped the lid on the coffee cup and placed it on the counter before Lacy.

"It's a sub. That Panino crap is snobbish gobbledygook to triple the price." Lacy took a sip from her cup and hummed. "Christ, that's a good cup of coffee."

"You know none of this is free. It's deducted from my pay." Madison reached for the tong, clamped it on the Panino Lacy signalled, and walked it to the hot press. "You complain enough as it is about my meagre paycheque, and if you continue to eat it away, I'm never bringing home that executive salary you want."

Blue eyes steady on defiant blue eyes, Lacy looked at the face so much like hers. Madison's waist-long glossy black hair was pulled back into a ponytail, accentuating her heart-shaped face, with large, round eyes crowned with long, dark lashes. Madison's face had the silky smoothness of a twenty-two-year-old, which Lacy, at seventeen years her senior, had lost to lines etched by a hard life.

Madison was lean with a fit frame, a genetic trait Lacy or possibly her father had handed down—if she knew who he was. Madison was five-eight, four inches taller than her mother. She wore her customary jeans, a white T-shirt, and scuffed running shoes from many years of use.

Lacy sighed. "Oh, honey, I stopped expecting anything of any consequence from you long ago."

Madison set the bagged Panino on the counter. "Well, ditto, Mother dearest."

Lacy's smile spread wide at Madison's sharp tongue, which came from her side of the family. "Touché daughter, touché."

Despacito segued into Paris by The Chainsmokers. Some in the crowd mouthed the words to the song, and Lacy's eyebrows furrowed. Music died a gruesome death after the eighties.

"Raisin cinnamon bagel, toasted with butter, Madison," Mike called out from the cash register.

Madison acknowledged the order with a "Coming up."

Wiping her hands dry on the front of the green apron emblazoned with the words *The Coffee Shop*, Madison slid on a pair of disposable gloves. Reaching for the bagel, she cut it in half with the serrated knife and set it to toast.

"What's that?" Madison asked when Lacy set the papers on the counter.

"Those are copies of the monthly bills. You're going to start contributing to the household expenses, Maddie. I've carried you for long enough."

Madison sucked in air and hissed it out. Her mother could be such a depressant injector. "Can we have this conversation later, Mother? As you can see, I'm swamped right now." She put the bagel with two containers of butter, a plastic knife, and a napkin into a paper bag and handed it to the girl in the green and burgundy plaid uniform scrolling through her cell phone. The girl didn't acknowledge or thank Madison. That was the sum of her life.

"Whether we talk about it now or later, the outcome is the same. You're an adult now and need to pay your way, and you're contributing to the household expenses." Lacy reached into her tote, and Madison assumed her mother was going for her cigarettes.

"I told you, you can't smoke in here? You think as a nurse you'd know better." Madison hooked the tongs onto a blueberry muffin and bagged it. Pointing at table five, she signalled to pick up the bag.

"I was reaching for the additional bills, internet, taxes, and miscellaneous to add to the pile."

"Madison, two Grande coffees, a scone with peanut butter, and a strawberry cake lollipop." Mike handed the young pimpled face kid change from a ten-dollar bill. "All separate orders."

Madison reached for two cups and flipped the handle on the urn to let the coffee pour. "You know I make a pittance and can barely make ends meet. How am I supposed to contribute to pay the bills?"

Lacy watched her daughter manage the multiple orders with ease. If only Madison would put her skills to better use. "You'll have to figure it out. It's about time you carried your weight. We're splitting costs fifty-fifty."

Madison slammed the two coffee cups on the counter. "I can't afford that, and you make way more money than I do at this crappy job." She wouldn't dare tell her mother that much of her pay cheque went toward paying for the private investigator working for her for the past seven months. That wasn't a conversation she was ready or willing to spar over with her mother.

"Madison, this," Mike raised a hand, palm out and circled it before Madison, "is not the attitude we want to convey to our customers. There's too much negativity there."

Madison turned and flashed Mike a forced all teeth smile. "Better?"

Mike's slash of dark eyebrows rose. "Right. Well, I need three regulars. Leave room for cream."

"Go away, Mother. You're funking up my workspace and generating too much negativity in peaceful Madison."

Lacy rolled her eyes dramatically and reached for the bag containing the Panino. "This is my dinner, so make arrangements for yours," she said as Amber Fox-Roche flashed on the television screen.

The words to her lauded, syndicated show Tell Me All appeared on the screen before fading, and the camera closed in on her. Amber's straight, black hair was perfectly groomed, and her makeup was expertly applied. Her large, cerulean eyes were dusted in bronze, her high cheekbones rouged, and her full lips traced in dark plum lipstick. Her nails were long, painted salmon-pink on manicured hands.

Amber wore diamond studs at her ears, a gold chain around her long neck, gold bangle bracelets on her wrist, and a gold wedding band encrusted with diamonds. The sharp red suit she wore with matching stilettos suited her tall, slim frame and added to the poised, confident image she portrayed on camera. On the matching gray chair beside Amber, handsome Keanu Reeves up-talked the newly released John Wick movie. Amber smiled with all her warmth and force.

The epitome of manufactured perfection, Lacy thought, staring at Amber. As beautiful as Amber was on the outside, she was morally corrupt on the inside. Or was the term moral turpitude more apt? The public would know who the real Amber Fox-Roche was if Madison told all.

Lacy flicked her eyes from the television toward her daughter, who had stopped what she was doing and transfixed her eyes on Amber. The look on Madison's face was a worrisome cagey stare out of blue eyes.

Nothing good came from that look.

Chapter 2

SAMANTHA HALLSTEAD WAS the complete package. Samantha had steel-blue eyes, long legs that never seemed to end, and a curvy body that never quit—literally. She advocated for great sex and enjoyed it as often as possible. Because that's what men are for, she said in response to Amber's probing of her liberal lifestyle.

Samantha Hallstead was intelligent, independent, and opinionated. She went by Sam Hallstead purely for entertainment purposes. She enjoyed the expression triggered in clients and adversaries who assumed Sam was a man and instead got a flaming red-haired goddess with menacing blue eyes.

Since Sam and Amber met in drama class during their first year of high school, the two women became besties and were inseparable. Sam and Amber did everything together and vowed to one another to pursue careers behind the camera.

However, along the way, Sam's umpteenth boyfriend gave her a taste for the law, and she redirected her life's ambition. The news was a great relief to Amber, who felt Sam would be a formidable adversary, and she'd lose every time in the ratings.

Sam was the stronger of the two. Sam was more competitive, more cunning, and more ruthless. Friends or not, Sam's ultimate goal was to win no matter what.

Amber didn't resent Sam for it. It was how she was wired. It was why Sam Hallstead was known in prosecution circles as The Piranha. It was why Sam formed and ran Hallstead Law at thirty-three, with thirty employees and generated millions of dollars in revenue.

Sam was single by choice. She didn't believe in monogamy or sharing her money with any man. Sam was eternally grateful to the feminists before her who'd challenged prevailing attitudes toward women and afforded her the privilege to live as she did.

From Sappho to Gloria Steinem, Sam was sure each would concur with her belief that her hard-earned money was hers to spend as she liked, unlike Amber, who was happy to support her useless, mooching husband and continued to finance Carpaccio Ristorante, his money-draining dream.

"So, things are ... good?" Sam watched Amber walk across the shiny, white marble floor to the glass wall that presented a panoramic view of the colourful gardens and the green roll of the land. Straight ahead was the lake, where two white swans skirted along the water carving a path.

Sliding the doors open, Amber breathed in the perfumes of spring floating in the air from the gardens in glorious bloom. The late afternoon sun washed out of a cloudless sky and spilled into the living room, lighting it bright.

The room was a cozy oasis of ivory walls, long white sofas, reclaimed wood tables, and the console table crowded with framed photographs of her family and daughter Lily.

"Why do you always ask the same thing?" Amber leaned a shoulder against the doorframe and watched

Hunter, her husband, throw the ball to Lily. "Yes, things are great. They've never been better." With a beaming smile, Amber watched her boisterous five-year-old daughter, with an abundance of energy, chase after the ball and kicked it to her father, laughing as she did.

"I'm happy for you, Amber, that you got your shit together." Sam tucked her legs up under her and leaned back on the sofa.

"Don't ever let it be said lawyers aren't articulate." Amber made her way to the sofa and sat beside Sam with Bessie, the white and brown Ba-Shar, between them.

The smirk twisted Sam's lips. "Damn straight."

"Bessie, go outside to play with Lily." Amber got a droopy raised eye from Bessie. "I had to get the laziest dog at the pound. Move, Bessie, and get your ass outside. Go on." When the dog didn't budge, Amber rose and gestured for Bessie to follow her to the door. Once there, she waved hands to encourage the dog outside onto the terrace. Amber waited as Bessie weighed the benefits of going out. "Go on," she said, stepping out the door, hoping the dog would mimic her.

Bessie took a moment longer to debate before she walked outside, strolled across the terrace, down the stairs, and belly-flop onto the grass.

"That's one lazy dog," Amber murmured with a smile.

"Makes you wonder who the master is." Sam waved her empty glass at Amber, signalling her to bring the Zinfandel bottle to the sofa. Sam gave Amber a half-amused look when she did as told.

"I love watching Hunter and Lily play. He loves that little girl so much. He's become a different person since Lily came into our life. He's loving, caring, and so involved, not to mention thoughtful. Just yesterday, he showed up with a bouquet of roses for me and a bouquet of lilies for Lily, her favourite flower." Amber aimed her eyes at the overflowing vases on the console table.

"They're lovely."

"The inexplicable powers of a child's love."

"Yes, the inexplicable powers of a child's love."

As close a friend as Sam was to Amber, as well as she knew her, she wouldn't voice her true thoughts. How did you tell someone you loved that the glue that held her relationship together was their child and nothing else? Amber was so in love with Hunter that it blinded her to his shortcomings, and she forgave him for his indiscretions.

Hunter was a horndog before Amber met him, and he would continue to be one until he reached the fires of hell. Because once a horndog, always a horndog. Why couldn't Amber see that as clearly as Sam did? Love, Sam thought, blinded you, cut off your sense of smell and diminished common sense.

Why Amber, a strong, intelligent, successful woman, allowed her heart to rule over her common sense boggled Sam. Sam would never let herself fall into that trap. Luckily for Sam, she was in no danger of falling under any man's spell. She was too self-centred for that to happen.

Selfishness was an underrated trait.

"Hunter comes straight home from the restaurant and spends as much time as he can with us here at home." Amber refreshed Sam's drink and hers. "You can set the toppled hamster in your head, back onto the wheel."

"He never fell off, and good to know," Sam said, but Amber heard so much more.

"And the sex is ... incredible."

It should be. He's had enough variety in his life to perfect it. "That's great."

Again, Amber heard Sam's judgment, saw the withering scorn in her eyes, and gave her a sidelong glance. "Why can't you try to like Hunter? He's been nothing but good to you, even after the way you treat him."

There's nothing to like. "I'm trying my best."

Annoyance flicked briefly in Amber's eyes. "Try harder." Amber reached for Sam's hand. "Please, Sammy. You're my best friend, and I need you to get along with my husband."

Hope was an eternal spring in Amber. If Sam hadn't been able to get along with the man during their ten years of marriage, Amber should accept that the ship had long sailed to the point of no return.

"I will. I promise." Sam looked away from Amber's hard, unwavering eyes. "And who's this beautiful girl?" Sam said when Lily came running into the room with Hunter and Bessie following.

Bessie wore purple tights, a pink-ribbed top, and matching running shoes. Her hair was tied into curly pigtails with ribbons. Lily was adorable, lovable, and the closest thing to a niece Sam would have.

"Auntie Sam," Lily shrieked and jumped into Sam's arms. "Did you bring me a present?"

"Lily, what have I said about that?"

"Sorry, Mommy, but Auntie Sam always brings me the best presents." Lily pushed her lower lip out, slightly pouted and aimed the large, round, dark eyes that melted her mother's heart in her direction.

She was her child, Amber thought, brushing her lips over the chestnut hair with motherly love. "Still, asking for things we haven't earned is not polite. Agree?"

"Agreed, Mommy." Lily nodded, and her pigtails bounced.

"Speaking of asking for things you haven't earned, how are you, Hunter?" Sam asked, avoiding Amber's slitted gaze.

"I'm good, Sam. Haven't seen you at the restaurant parading the boy-toy-slash-victim du-jour?"

Taking a sip of her wine, Sam studied Hunter over the rim of her glass. He wore black Gucci loafers, charcoal pants, a cream polo shirt, collar up—douche style. His hair was thick and black as coal, his mouth wide. He had sea-blue eyes and bore a fashionable stubble on his square jaw. He was a couple of inches short of six feet, with a muscular frame and the indefinable hint of sensuality a woman liked in a man. Wasted good looks on a douche and certainly not the look you'd expect of a chef.

Sam opened her mouth but closed it when Lily jumped on the sofa beside her. "As Mommy said, it isn't polite to ask for things, but Auntie Sam wouldn't dare come see her favourite girl without a gift."

"What is it? What is it? What did you get me?" Lily said excitedly.

Amber framed her daughter's face with her hands. "Stop harassing Auntie Sam. The present is upstairs in your room. Take Bessie with you," Amber said when Lily jumped off the sofa.

"Okay, Mommy. Come on, Bessie. We're going to get my present."

Amber caught Lily's arm before she turned to go. "What do you say to Auntie Sam, young lady?"

"Thank you, Auntie Sam." Lily pecked Sam's cheek. "And thanks, Mommy, for letting me keep my present." Lily wrapped her arms around her mother, and Amber embraced her tightly.

Sam saw the pure love between mother and child that radiated across the space between them, and it arrowed into her heart. Although Sam had opted out of motherhood long ago, she wondered if she could nurture such a loving connection with a child of hers.

"I'll go with Lily to see if the present you gave her is suitable for a child." Hunter emptied the whiskey in his glass and turned to follow his daughter.

Caustically, Sam smiled. "Impersonating a moral person doesn't suit you, Hunter."

"I wish I could say it was a pleasure, Sam. You're welcome to show your way out at any time," Hunter called out on his way out of the living room.

Amber huffed out a breath. "Honestly, what am I to do with the two of you? Don't make me choose, Sam, because, in the end, he's my husband," Amber said flatly.

Sam tilted back the wine glass for a long sip. "Both you and I know you'd never choose between us."

Amber smiled a little. "No, I wouldn't. It's why you need to try to get along with Hunter."

"Fine. Okay. I promise I'll try harder." Sam vowed, and Amber looked at her in an odd sort of triumph.

A bottomless well of hope was Amber.

Chapter 3

"SERIOUSLY, KAREN, YOU think the one dollar and seventy-five cents you're spending gives you this voice?" said Madison from behind the cash register with a rebuking look at the woman with the blonde bob.

Many queued behind the middle-aged entitled woman snickered, fuelling her anger.

"For one, my name's not Karen. Two, I demand to speak to the manager." Karen's smug grin flattened when instead of support, the coffee shop patrons burst into laughter. Some made a little snorting laugh.

"Of course you do. Christ, lady, you're the epitome of a Karen," said one.

"Can you feel more entitled?" said another.

"Lady, you give Karens a bad name," said the young girl behind her, holding her cell phone up in record mode. The approval followed.

"Now, Karen," Madison strung out the name for emphasis, "get to the back of the line where you should be or get out of the store. We don't need your attitude here." Madison's firm finger pointed to the door.

The room clapped, some cheered.

"I... I...." Karen groped for words. Feeling the need to regain her dignity, Karen slammed the counter with the palm of her hands and leaned closer so her face was inches from Madison's. "I demand to see your manager."

Some jeered, and many laughed with their cell phones held in the air.

"Shit." Stepping out of the storeroom, Mike walked into the hostile atmosphere, dropped the box in his arms and rushed to Madison's side. "Ma'am, I'm the manager. How may I help you?"

"There you go, Karen. Your revered god, the manager," said the young woman in line behind her. "Go off on your complaint. Hurry it up. Some people have places to get to."

"Again, my name's not Karen," she said over her shoulder and then turned to Mike. "You can help by firing this insolent girl right now." Now, the entitlement seemed to feed on itself.

The young man sitting at the round table with the Bieber hair sweep shot to his feet. "Hey, boomer, shut the fuck up. The cashier's in the right. You're the one who waltzed past everyone and cut to the front of the line as if you were Gaga or something." He flashed his cell phone at the woman. "See, I've got you on camera doing exactly that."

Remarks of agreement followed from everyone in the café, as did the flashing cell phones.

"I'm a paying customer. I'm in here every day," Karen asserted.

"And that gives you the right to barge in like an entitled Karen-tank?" asked someone from the depths of the room.

"You better not be putting that up on the interwebs," the woman said, and many in the room moved to press the send button. "I'll sue everyone one of you."

"You do that, Karen," said one.

"You're in a public space," said another.

"Look, I already have twenty-five likes, but not in the way you think, Karen," said a third person.

Mike injected himself into the conversation. "Jesus, Madison, I leave you for a few minutes alone and...."

Karen cut Mike off. "I want her fired," she said with a hard stare.

Madison's lips slanted into a sneer. "Yeah, because a daily coffee purchase gives you ultimate control over everyone's life."

"Shut up, Madison," Mike barked.

Karen said, "Yes, shut up, Madison."

"You shut up, Karen. You too, ball-less manager," one said.

"You shut up," Karen shot back.

Mike cautiously entered the conversation and said, "Ma'am, that's unnecessary," to de-escalate the situation.

"She started this. Do you know how much money I've spent in this dump?" Ice dripped from Karen's words.

"I know you're a loyal customer, and I'll do anything necessary to right this." Mike flashed his best magnetic managerial smile.

"Jesus, Mikey, grow a pair." Bieber-sweep sitting at the round table said in disgust.

Mike filled a cup and handed it to Karen. "Please, take this on the house and anything else you'd like." Mike's words came out shaky, but some of his panic eased when he saw Karen's thoughtful, narrow-eyed look, which told him she was considering taking him up on his offer.

"All right. I'll take a plain bagel, toasted with butter. Three butter containers, not the usual stingy two you give. Two's not enough. And I'll take a Parmesan Scone and a blueberry muffin. To go," Karen said.

"Yes, of course, right away, ma'am. Madison, get the lady her order," Mike instructed.

"Yeah, no, that's not going to happen. I quit." Madison untied her apron and tossed it at Mike.

Over the cheering from customers, Mike's voice rose to a screeching shriek. "What do you mean you quit? You're in the middle of your shift, and we're busy off our feet here."

"I'm out of here because you, Mike, make this place a toxic work environment for us employees. For the pittance I make, I don't need to deal with you or this Karen here."

"You go nuclear on his ass, girl," said one patron.

"You're damn straight I am." Madison reached for her handbag under the counter and flipped up the pass-through. "And, lady, don't forget that you have one foot in the grave, and hell is as miserable a place as you make people's lives with a manager who isn't as accommodating as Mike the ball-less-wonder."

Claps and comments of support followed Madison out the door.

"Word, Madison."

"Power to you."

"You colour outside the line, baby."

Chapter 4

LACY WALKED TO the kitchen of her small condominium. It was neat and orderly. Oak cupboards were polished to a shine, and the smell of lemon pledge painted the air. The stainless steel appliances sparkled, the counters were clear of clutter, and the tile floor shone. Lacy might be many things, but messy she was not. It was a by-product of her nursing training.

"You got fired." Lacy stood at the kitchen counter, looking at her daughter.

Madison fell back onto the sofa. "No, Mother, I told you I walked out. This Karen was going off on me, and I didn't deserve her unwarranted anger, and that asshole Mike wouldn't support me. That place is so toxic."

Reaching into the cupboard for the brandy bottle, Lacy poured it into a tall glass and sent brandy streaming down her throat. "You're not in a financial position that allows you to have an opinion or make statements. You can barely make ends meet."

Madison tipped back her head and closed her eyes. "I'll get another job."

"This is the fourth job you've had in eighteen months. You need to get your shit together, Madison. You're not a kid anymore."

Madison ignored the jab. "Goes to show that I can easily find another job. I'll have a glass of brandy."

"No, you may not. You can't afford it." Lacy walked the bottle and the glass to the living room and sat beside Madison on the sofa. "A monkey can get hired at a minimum wage job."

"They should give licences to breed, or at least a mothering certificate." Madison pushed off the sofa. There were times she couldn't stand to be in the same room with her mother, and now was one of those times.

"Remember, as of next month, we're splitting expenses right down the middle. So, you better come up with a solution soon." She stretched out her legs on the glass coffee table.

Madison paused at the door and looked back. "I already have, Mom."

"What are you going to do?"

"What I should have done long ago." Madison straightened her shoulders and walked out of the room.

"What does that mean, Maddie? Madison Donnell, get back here and tell me what exactly that means," Lacy demanded, and Madison's response was a hard slam of her bedroom door.

Chapter 5

MADISON WAS UP early the following day. Showered, she threw on the sunflower-yellow dress she picked up at Goodwill for today. Her dark, long hair fountained down to her waist. She wore Birkenstock Sandals—another Goodwill find. Madison dabbed a layer of pink lip gloss on her lips for the occasion.

Today, first impressions were essential.

Madison headed out the door before her mother was up.

Madison's drive from her downtown Toronto apartment to the northern suburb of Richmond Hill was a slow, bumper-to-bumper drive that took ninety minutes. Reaching her destination, Madison maneuvered the car onto Regent Street and saw what she expected.

It was an upscale neighbourhood with large-scale, high-priced homes with a lot of land safeguarded by tall wrought-iron fences. Exquisitely tailored green lawns levelled at precisely three inches hemmed professionally landscaped gardens overflowing with vibrant and aromatic spring blooms. Hundred-year-old trees lined the street; sunlight seeped through small breaks in their canopy.

There were homes with wraparound porches and stylish teak furniture covered with floral cushions. Other houses had regal portico entrances with tall columns, double-carved oak doors, climbing vines, and slate walkways. All had cobbled circular driveways.

Madison stopped in front of 42 Regent Street. The two-story white stucco, modern-looking flat roof home had a predominant Frank Lloyd influence. Double entrance glass doors, interlaced with wrought-iron and large picture windows framed black, faced the circular driveway.

The entry gate to the property was open, and Madison steered the car into the driveway and parked in front of the stone fountain dripping water from basin to basin. At its base, the flowerbed popped with white and purple tulips.

Killing the car's engine, Madison remained silent. For a long moment, she watched the house. It was a stunning home in idyllic surroundings. She'd never be able to afford anything as grand.

Madison hated rich people.

Madison wasn't greedy. She'd settle for rich-adjacent living, and if her plan went as planned, Madison was about to realize that and live like a rich woman in a grand home.

Doubt had Madison rethinking her game plan. "What am I doing here?"

Her eyes peeled out the car's windshield. Madison watched the two blue jays wing across the blue sky and land on the maple tree. Three Starlings followed the blue jays and perched above them. From somewhere, a woodpecker pecked, and the blue jays and starlings launched into birdsong.

For a moment, Madison thought she was in the midst of a movie where the ending was always perfect and happy. But she wasn't in a film, and it wasn't a perfect or happy moment. It was what Madison had to do, what she needed to do.

As much as Madison felt she was putting her life into the hands of a stranger, she had to do it.

"You'll be fine. You've been planning this for months. Go with the script you've burned to memory. You can do this," Madison told herself.

Opening the car's door, Madison smoothed the front of her sundress and pinched her cheeks for colour. She took a deep breath and started for the front door as two female joggers in purple leggings, tank tops, and white running shoes ran past the sidewalk. Both joggers wore headbands and a fanny pack around their waists, and their faces gleamed with a thin layer of sweat. From behind the dark shade of sunglasses that cost more than Madison's car, the two women gave her a suspicious look. Madison supposed her dilapidated Civic got their attention. Anything less than a Jaguar on Regal Street alerted the residents of the lower-class intrusion.

At the front door, Madison agonized. Should she knock? Should she walk away? Madison rolled the pros and cons in her head.

What would she find? She was curious to see what she looked like in person. She'd be interfering in her life, a disruptive force, an unnecessary upheaval in her ideal life.

Madison's courage was fading fast, and on a shaky breath, she turned to walk away.

"Can I help you?" said the woman who opened the door.

Madison swirled to face the woman arched in the door. She wore a lime-green sleeveless dress with a wide belt. The gold buckle of the Gucci belt glistened under the sunlight. Her dark, silky hair was tied in a stylish bun. Her almond-shaped eyes were dusted with soft pink eyeshadow, her cheeks in rosy-rouge, and her lips painted cherry red. She was tall and lean, with well-defined arms. The woman worked out a lot. Amber Fox-Roche was gorgeous, stylish, graceful, and the embodiment of confidence.

Madison felt awkward in her Goodwill outfit and the Dollar Store makeup.

"You've been standing here for some time loitering at my front door." Amber jutted her chin up to the camera. "Either you tell me what you want, or I'll have to call the police," she said in the pleasant, dignified voice of the wealthy.

Madison had never been at a loss for words as she was now. Taking a deep breath, Madison tried to relax. You can do this, Madison. You have to. "My name's Madison." Madison's voice was calm, but the spear of panic still sliced through her.

"And what is it you want, Madison?"

Madison caught a whiff of Amber's perfume, sweet-smelling and expensive. Money bought outward class, Madison thought. "My name's Madison...."

"You said that already." Amber sipped from the coffee cup in her hand—the words World's Best Mom printed in bold, red burned in Madison's eyes.

"My name's Madison Donnell. I'm Lacy Donnell's daughter. Nurse Lacy Donnell." Madison waited for that to sink in. It took seconds, and when it did, Amber drained of colour, and her eyes grew huge. She lost her grip on the cup, and it fell onto the stone steps. Liquid splattered and ceramic pieces scattered at her feet. "Are you all right?"

"I'm fine." Amber's control was back, although she didn't have as tight a grip on it as it appeared.

"You recognize the name?" Madison asked.

Aber lowered her head and bent down to pick up the broken pieces at her feet with trembling hands. "No. No, I don't.

"I think you do, and I know what you did in the fall of twenty-twelve. It was me who shared the room with you."

"Shit." Amber sliced her finger open. Blood spurted on her dress as she brought her finger to her mouth. "You need to go," she said, sucking down on her finger.

"If I leave now, I'm heading straight to your competitor from Channel 8. I'm sure Patty McLeod will be more than happy to listen to what I have to say. I'm sure she'd be more than happy to hear what I have to say."

The hum, forceful and steady, buzzed in Amber's head. Her stomach rolled and threatened to expel that morning's breakfast. Unable to speak, Amber stared at Madison with wide eyes.

"What's it going to be, the great Amber Fox-Roche? Talk to me now or go to your competition and spill my guts."

Chapter 6

AMBER STEPPED ASIDE to let Madison into her home. Walking in, Madison surveyed the house with a look that took every detail of its appearance.

Like its exterior, the home's interior was modern and stylish. Straight lines, high ceilings, white walls, dark wood floors, and clear banisters with iron railings dominated the look. Abstract paintings flowing with vivid colours hung on the walls.

An oversize vase on the black lacquer table at the centre of the oval foyer overflowed with freshly picked spring flowers. To the right was the study with walls covered in bookcases jammed with books. Crafted Parnian furniture, a desk, chairs, and a sofa filled the room. The television above the fireplace broadcasted the hour's show on Amber's network. A straight staircase to the left led to the four bedrooms and four bathrooms. Above that was another floor with more bedrooms, bathrooms, a family room, and a study.

Amber led Madison past the entry hall toward the back to the combined living room, kitchen and dining room. From top to bottom and end to end, the back wall was glass and showed a clear view of the gardens, pool with the sun slanting along the surface, deflecting and shimmering, and tennis court.

Lake Ruby came into view a hundred yards up the flat green terrain. Its water was a black mirror, and a few swans and ducks glided across its smooth surface. The lake was oblong shaped and ringed by grand homes with lots of glass to get a view of the picturesque surroundings.

To the right, Madison saw the guesthouse. It was twice the size of her mother's six-hundred-square-foot apartment. A copse of tall maple and fir trees ringed it and protected it from the westerly winds. On the small porch, above two red Muskoka chairs and matching table, hanging baskets spilled with pink and white Bougainville.

There, Madison decided, was where she was going to live.

Madison turned to Amber and watched her trash the broken ceramic pieces in her hand into the garbage. "This is an impressive place."

Amber didn't hear Madison and didn't turn to face her. Instead, she lowered her head and closed her eyes, trying to rid herself of the scream piercing her skull.

As much as Amber wished this day wouldn't come, she knew it eventually would.

Fuck, and double fuck.

Amber did everything possible to cover up what transpired that summer. She ensured nothing actionable and no paper or money trail was left behind. Sam didn't know what had happened that summer, and Amber had never told her.

Amber had carried her secret inside her all this time, tormenting and eating at her like a corrosive acid. She had been careful and discreet to avoid it touching her personal and professional life and her family—specifically Hunter, who'd leave her if he knew.

Yet here it was, upending her life in her home.

Amber sucked in air through her mouth and exhaled through her nose. "What do you want? Money?" There was hesitation in her voice. Bribes led to a bottomless pit of demands, but desperation called for irrationality.

"No, I don't want money, per se," said Madison.

Amber whirled to Madison. The despairing look on Amber's face told Madison it was not the response she had hoped for.

The fear and distress welling up inside threatened to choke Amber. "Just say what you want."

"Aren't you adorable," Madison said when Bessie came running in through the doggie door and gave a bark of introduction. "Yes, you are." Bessie rose on her hind legs to greet Madison, and she delighted the dog with head scratches.

"I don't want to disrupt your or your family's life. All I ask for is room and board and a job." Madison fell back into the long sofa. The cushions were buttery soft, a far cry from the brick-hard sofa her mother bought from the local discount furniture outlet.

Whoever said money couldn't buy happiness was never poor.

Amber walked to the bar and reached for the cognac bottle and a glass. "I don't have a job to offer, and you sure as hell can't stay here." She drank half the cognac in a single pull.

Madison draped her arms on the back of the sofa and stared at Amber with the fierceness of a hunter looking its prey in the eyes. "I was thinking of becoming your nanny. You know, taking care of Lily when you're at work, which is always. You're a hard-working lady."

Amber drank the rest of her cognac in one swallow.

"I can take care of your home." Madison patted the cushion for the dog to climb on the sofa, and Bessie happily obliged. "I can cook and clean. This is a huge house with lots to clean." Madison set her eyes on the massive flat-screen television on the wall.

Glaring eyes stared back. "I already have someone who comes in daily to do that." Amber poured more cognac.

"Great, so I'll just be a nanny." Madison crossed one slender leg over another. "Is the guest house at the back empty?" Understanding where the conversation was heading, Amber took a sizeable, numbing gulp of cognac. "I thought I could move in. I hope it's furnished because I can't afford to do it myself."

Silence.

Amber's cell phone rang from somewhere in the room and pinged for the tenth time. She didn't move to answer it.

"I know this all comes as a shock, Amber. May I call you Amber?" The thunderous silence drifted for a while. "Anyway, Amber, I hate doing this, but it's something I must do."

Amber gave in to temper and impulse. "You're not going to get what you want. This charade of yours is ending now."

"I don't think you're in a position to make threats, Amber, not unless you want to destroy your career and this sweet life, which I can do with one phone call. What I know of Amber Fox-Roche is that she loves her comfortable, celebrity lifestyle." Madison pushed to her feet. "I'm a reasonable woman. I've waited this long and can wait a few more days. Let your husband know I'll be moving in by the end of the week." Madison ran a hand over Bessie's head. "It was nice to meet you, perfect doggie in the perfect home with the perfect mommy."

Bessie gave a happy bark before scampering through the doggie door.

"I'll walk myself out." Madison stopped at the door. "As I said, I don't want to do this, Amber. It's something I must do because of your doing. Some things cannot be forgiven, and some actions are impossible to forget. And what you did is repugnant, beyond the pale, and fundamentally deceitful. And now it's payback."

Chapter 7

MADISON TOSSED THE last of her clothes into the duffel bag. Turning back to the dresser that was as old as she was, Madison scanned the drawers one last time. All of her worldly possessions were in one duffel bag.

But things were about to change—for the better. Madison would live in a home surrounded by majestic trees next to a lake where swans swam.

Blackmail was such an unmusical word but so very profitable.

Madison was tired of a life that cascaded from one worry to the next, from paycheque to paycheque. At twenty-two, she was jaded, possibly to the point of no return, and her trust in humanity was non-existent. Betrayal had come long ago and touched her life with its keen edge of disillusionment.

Madison had her mother and Amber Fox-Roche to thank for that.

It might be false hope, and Madison's blackmail scheme against Amber might blow up in her face, but it had to be done. Amber had to pay for what she did.

Madison set the bottle of Eau de Toilette back down on the dresser. She would leave it for her mother. Madison wouldn't be using inexpensive Eau de Toilette anymore. She wouldn't be using cheap anything, for that matter. Amber owed her that much.

The scent of coffee had Madison turning toward the door to see Lacy standing at the bedroom door with two white mugs. A mist of steam curled from the mugs in her hands. "I thought you could use a cup."

Madison zipped up the duffel bag. "Since when do you bring me coffee?"

"I'm trying to do something nice, Maddie." Lacy set the mug on the night table and sat on the edge of the bed.

Too little too late, Mother.

"Where are you going, Maddie?" Lacy said with a sweetness Madison knew she didn't possess.

"I'll let you know when I figure it out. For now, you can forward my mail to this P.O. box." Madison purposely set up the post office box to ensure her mother didn't track her to Amber's home or connect the dots. "I doubt you'll be paying my bills, so make sure you send them on time."

"Madison Donnell, you're broke and unemployed. How can you afford to go out on your own? Is there something you need to tell me?" Lacy's voice rose and hardened with impatience.

"There's nothing to tell, and I thought you'd be happy to see me go." Madison walked to the bathroom, picked up her toothbrush, hairbrush, hairdryer, and scrunchies, returned to the bedroom, and tossed them into her bag.

"Why would you say that? I like having you here."

"What you like, Mother, is to have me pick up half of your expenses."

"Don't be like that, Maddie."

"I'll no longer be the financial burden or so-called 'cursed albatross around your neck,' Mother." Madison threaded her arms into the red hoodie and zipped it up.

"Maddie, don't be so dramatic. When have I said that?"

"You didn't. You thought it every day of my existence and made me feel it."

Lacy opened her mouth to say something but realized it was best to say nothing and shut it.

"You're silence speaks volumes." Madison picked up the duffel bag off the bed. "Besides, now you can spend the two hundred thousand dollars in your bank account on yourself." Madison walked out on those words, leaving her mother with her mouth open in a stunned O.

Chapter 8

TODAY WASN'T GOING to be an ordinary day. Madison wouldn't be working at a crappy minimum wage job for a second-rate manager and dealing with entitled Karens whose lives were so empty and hollow that making people's life miserable fulfilled them.

Today Madison's new life began, and her cheeks flushed with pleasure.

With a satisfied smile, Madison surveyed the interior of her new home. Amber's guest home was quaint, airy, and stylish. The ground floor was an open space with a combination living room, dining room, and kitchen. The walls were pale gray, the floors polished hardwood, and the furnishings were minimalist but ample.

The living room's L-shaped charcoal sofa with matching ottoman sat on a cobalt rug. A flat-screen television hung above the tan marble fireplace. Adjacent was the dining room. A round glass table, four chairs, and a buffet table were all there was, all that was needed. Next to it, the kitchen was small but well equipped with stainless steel appliances, chocolate-brown millwork, and cream-coloured counters. There was an entry closet and a bathroom. Bright morning sunlight poured from the windows around the room.

It was perfect, and it was now home.

"There are two bedrooms upstairs," Amber said, watching Madison open and close the kitchen cupboards while Bessie followed closely.

Amber had taken the day off work for the second time in her career to deal with Madison. A rerun of Tell Me All aired today.

"Good, but it's not like I'm planning to have guests over except for you." Madison looked at Bessie, who excitedly smiled at her and swished her tail. "You are my only friend."

Two meetings and the dog would walk through fire for her, Amber thought. Amber would call the dog away if she didn't risk Bessie snubbing her. She could bribe Bessie with the biscuit in her jeans pocket, but that would seem obvious and pitiful. Madison was taking over Amber's life, and to what end?

"I'm not here to disrupt your life, Amber." Madison ran a hand over the smooth quartz countertop. "I'll need money, just enough to stock the shelves and the refrigerator. I'm not here to take advantage of you, either. All I ask is for a living income. By that, I mean in the style you're accustomed to."

Amber was smart enough to realize confrontation wouldn't play in her favour, and she pressed her lips together to hold in words.

"It's not too much to ask. Not after what you did." Madison said.

How long will this go on? Amber quietly wondered.

Madison levelled a look at Madison, who looked strangely underdressed in her lounging around clothes: skinny jeans, a scarlet shirt, and flat ballerina patent shoes. "I promise I'll be an excellent houseguest and will be the best nanny I can be for Lily."

What was she doing bringing Madison, a stranger, into her family and daughter's life? Amber reached into her jeans pocket for the cigarette pack and lighter.

"Nope, that's not happening in this house. For that matter, it's no longer happening inside the main house either or anywhere around Lily. Do you know what secondhand smoke does to a child's small lungs?"

"I actually don't smoke. I quit long ago." A faint flush of guilt coloured Amber's cheeks. "I just started…."

"When I appeared in the scene." Madison walked to the closet and hung up her hoodie on a hanger. "I appreciate I make you nervous. Regardless it stops now. I don't want that filthy habit around Lily. Agreed?"

Amber nodded. She felt like Playdough, moulded by the stranger who forced herself into her home.

"When does Lily get home?" Madison asked.

Amber felt her stomach muscles tighten, and her heart leaped to her throat.

"I'd like to meet her and have some time to get acquainted." Madison saw the worry flicker over Amber's face, and she said, "You can trust me with Lily, Amber. I haven't been around children, but I give you my word I'll look after her as if she was my own. I'm not here to upend her wonderful life. I have only her best interest at heart. Let me settle into my new home, and you can call me when she gets home."

Amber nodded as her stomach muscles wound into a tighter knot of nerves. She needed a stiff drink and a cigarette.

Chapter 9

MADISON LOOKED AT the child that ran toward Amber. She wore purple leggings with a unicorn print, a white polo shirt, and Gucci leather sneakers. Her eyes were dark as onyx and round as saucers. She had a tiny pug nose and a rosebud mouth. Her hair was bound into two pigtails with bright yellow ribbons. Lily was adorable and picture-perfect.

"I made this for you, Mommy." Lily handed Amber the canvas. "It's my hands. I made it with paint on my hands."

"It's beautiful, honey." Amber knelt so she could be at eye level with her daughter. "And I love the colours. It's very creative."

Lily shrugged. "I don't know what that means, but I liked squishing my hands in the paint. See?" She held her hands up, palms out to show her mother her paint-stained hands. "That's you, Bessie." Lily pointed on the drawing to a round brown dot with sticks for legs.

Bessie rose on her hind legs to inspect the drawing, barked her approval, and then stretched out on the floor.

"Bessie loves it, baby, as much as I do." Amber took the girl's hands and placed them on her face. "Paint my cheeks."

Lily giggled softly. "I can't, Mommy. My hands are dry now. Mrs. Star said the paint will come off after I wash my hands a few times."

"Yes, it will, baby."

Madison saw the love strong in Amber's eyes, heard it in her voice for the child, and a hard, unexpected wave of envy struck her. She had never seen that nurturing love in her mother for her.

"Hello," Lily said to Madison. "I'm Lily, like the flower. Who are you?"

"This is Madison, honey."

"Hello, Madison." Lily flashed Madison a dimpled smile.

"Hello, Lily. It's a pleasure to meet you finally. You are so much prettier in person than in the photographs I've seen of you," Madison said, never taking her eyes off Lily.

A shy smile played across Lily's face. "Thank you."

"Lily, Madison is going to be…."

"Sorry, we were late." Hunter cut Amber off when he walked into the kitchen. "Traffic was a nightmare. There's an accident…." He stopped when he saw Madison.

He wore pleated gabardine pants, gray. His shirt looked to be silk and expensive. His beard needed trimming but still looked fashionable. Hunter looked like he belonged in the centrefold of Fortune or GQ magazines.

Hunter's square, handsome face set in serious lines as he studied Madison. "You must be Madison." Hunter held out his hand, and Madison took it.

There was knowing in Hunter's sea-blue eyes, and Amber held a hint of suspicion. Trust after Hunter's indiscretion didn't come easily for Amber. It didn't help that Sam drilled in Amber's head the idea that Hunter went through women like a revolving door.

At Sam's insistence, Amber foolishly questioned Hunter, but refuting her suspicion was what Hunter did and did it well.

"Deny, deny, deny is the counter-offensive reaction of a guilty man. I'm a lawyer and know this first hand," Sam told Amber.

"That may be, but Hunter has denied having an affair, and I believe him, Sam. I know you have my best interest at heart, but please don't bring this up again," Amber said defiantly.

Amber was grateful Sam didn't raise the subject again because she was too ashamed to admit the truth.

Hunter didn't concede to the affairs, but Sam wasn't the only one who could detect guilt. As an interviewer, Amber's guilt-detecting radar recognized all the telltale signs in Hunter's denial of someone who wasn't telling the truth. If Hunter thought he could get away with the lie, he had another thing coming. Amber, after all, was an investigative reporter before hosting her primetime talk show, and the tools of the trade stuck with you.

Uncovering the crumbs Hunter left behind using her reporting skills didn't take long. Amber mined those crumbs and found what she didn't want to see. Amber discovered the missing money from the business account. She never dug deeper to find out who the women Hunter had an affair with were or how long the relationships lasted out of self-preservation. What you didn't know could hurt you, but before Amber stopped digging, she tracked the payments from Hunter to the doctor he paid for three separate discrete abortions, proving the affairs were real. Amber's breath caught in her throat.

Five years on, the shock still resonated in Amber.

After all the miscarriages she went through to conceive the child she wanted for them, finding out Hunter paid for the abortions to conceal his affair was a grenade to the system. Resentment bloomed into the anger Amber carried for Hunter. But then Amber became pregnant, and joy replaced anger. The baby inside her righted Amber's world, and she reasoned it would do the same for Hunter. Hunter would stop looking to fill the sad void inside him elsewhere. The baby would become the glue to bind them, and Hunter's lapse in judgment morphed into a forgotten memory for Amber.

"You two know one another?" Amber spoke calmly, but her eyes had storms in them.

"If I remember correctly, you went by Maddie then and worked at the restaurant as a server. Am I right?" Hunter hung his coat on the back of the bar stool perched by the kitchen island.

"Yes, on both counts. I was a terrible server and lasted only a few weeks." Madison walked to the refrigerator, reached for the milk, and poured it into a glass. "Would you like a cookie to go with that, Lily?"

"Yes, please. Shortbread, they're my favourite." Lily took the glass Madison held out to her.

"Coming right up, madam," Madison eyed the multitude of cupboard doors, "as soon as I figure out where they're hiding."

"Cookies don't hide. They're in there." Lily pointed to the door by the refrigerator leading into the pantry room.

Madison reached for the box of cookies and said to Lily, "I'll be booking an appointment with you to show me around this huge place of yours."

Lily's laugh sounded remarkably girlish. "You don't have to book an appointment with me. I live here."

"Me too," Madison said.

Lily's eyes rounded. "You do?"

"Yep, I've moved into the guesthouse and will take care of you. Would you like that?"

Madison saw Hunter's brows press together in puzzlement. "She is?" he mouthed to Amber.

Amber mouthed back, "We'll discuss it later."

"Yes, I'd like that. Will you play with me?" Lily said. "I have no one to play with. Mommy and Daddy won't give me a baby sister. Daddy plays with me when he's home, and so do Mommy and Auntie Sam, but they're not always home." Lily rambled on with a list of the games she liked to play. "Can I have three cookies? One's for Bessie. She likes shortbread too."

"Three cookies are coming right up, and I am happy to say I will play with you every chance. You'll have to teach me how to play the games you like." Madison set three cookies on a plate and walked them to the coffee table by the sofa.

"Sure," Lily said, following Madison.

Madison indicated Lily sit on the sofa. Lily did, and Bessie jumped up beside her. "My name is Madison, and I'll be your server tonight," she said, spreading a tea towel across Lily's lap and setting the plate down. "If you need anything else, ma'am, wave for me. Enjoy your snack, and don't forget to tip big."

"But I have no money." Lily handed Bessie her cookie, who took it in one bite.

Madison tapped the tip of Lily's nose. "A big smile will do." Lily flashed a huge smile. Madison touched the underside of her chin with her fingertips. "That one will count as two days' tips." She turned to Hunter. "She looks like you, Mr. Roche."

"Yes. Yes, she does." Hunter turned to Amber. "If you'll excuse us, I need to speak with my wife."

"Knock yourself out. I'm not going anywhere." Madison sat next to Lily. "What's your entertainment of choice, madam?" Madison said, reaching for the television remote.

Chapter 10

IN THE STUDY, away from Madison's listening ears, Hunter levelled his eyes at Amber. "You didn't tell me she was moving into the guest house."

Amber turned the lamps on and opened the blinds to illuminate the room. "I told you Madison would be Lily's full-time nanny. Full-time-nanny implies living here," Amber said, knowing well she purposely twisted her words when she told Hunter about hiring Madison to delay the conversation they were about to have.

"Why do you suddenly need a full-time nanny? We've been doing fine without one. Lily has school and daycare. She has enough care already."

Amber watched Hunter cross to the bar cart to pour himself a drink. "You and I are working long hours, and Lily's getting to the age where she needs to get out more often to expand her abundance of energy. Madison will take her for walks and to the park and entertain and give a growing girl the one-on-one attention she needs."

"I don't like it, Amber. We don't need a stranger in our home. Is she even qualified to be a nanny?" Hunter drank half the whisky in a single pull and refilled the glass. "She was a shit server. The worst. Caring for a child is way more demanding."

"She has her qualifications." Amber lied. "And you heard Lily, we're not always here, and she needs company. With Madison, we won't need to worry about who will rush out from work to pick her up. Best of all, Madison will give you and me peace of mind because I'm confident she will take good care of Lily."

Hunter knocked the second drink back, and Amber's face puzzled at his increasing agitation. "How well do you know this woman, Amber? Did you even vet her? I didn't when I hired her since I was desperate for a server, and you see how that ended."

"She'll be fine, and it seems Lily's taken a ... shine to her."

"Still, I don't want a stranger in my home and around my daughter."

Amber gave Hunter a stern look. "It's my home too, and she is my daughter."

"Yes, she is, but I'm putting my foot down on this. I don't want that ... woman in my home and around my daughter. Get rid of her, Amber."

Bewilderment was quickly replaced with suspicion, and Amber let her mind be carried toward the irrational.

Why was Hunter so opposed to Madison? Her illogical mind raced. They knew each other. Did they know each other beyond employer and employee? Amber's mind leaped into the unsound. Hunter and Madison's relationship went beyond work, and Madison was the woman Hunter had an affair with.

Reacting impulsively, jealous anger spit from Amber's eyes, and she barked, "Why are you reacting this way? I thought you'd be on board with a trustworthy person caring for our daughter. Do you know how difficult it is to find someone you can trust with your child?"

Hunter didn't have to read Amber's thoughts. Her tensing shoulders and the wild green-eyed look in her eyes told him all he needed to know. Hunter had to tame the get-out-of-my-bed stare and prevent her from cutting access to her money. The restaurant was a money pit, and Hunter couldn't afford to be separated from Amber's bank account.

Swallowing his pride, Hunter went into grovel mode. "I like how it is now, just the three of us." He walked to Amber and stroked his hand down her hair in a casually intimate way, making her pulse race. "Having a stranger in the house changes the … dynamics," he said with a quiet frankness to embellish his performance.

As Amber always did after their arguments, she regretted her emotional outburst and felt irritated with herself for being overly sensitive. She was a grown woman acting like a child.

Remorse washed over her, and Amber sighed deeply. "I'm sorry, baby. Sometimes I let my mind wander too much."

"This has Sam written all over it. You must top listening to her and allowing her to put all these crazy ideas in your head." He put a hand under her chin and lifted her face so their eyes met. "I love you and the family you gave me."

Amber bit her lip. "I know. I'm sorry, baby."

"Maybe you need to consider going back to counselling."

She flinched as if she'd been stung and made a noncommittal sound. The guilt of concealing from Hunter that she signed on for counselling to deal with the knowledge of the abortions and the stress of keeping it from public consumption was overwhelming. Amber couldn't return to that and couldn't risk damaging her reputation and losing her job and show. She had worked too hard and sacrificed much to get where she was, and she wouldn't give it all up because she acted like a jealous teenager.

"I'll think about it," Amber said.

"Okay." Hunter brushed his lips over hers. "You and I have something great going on. I'm sorry I overreacted, but what did you expect when you didn't read me in on this Madison thing? I wish you wouldn't have sprung this on us, on me, out of the blue. You understand that, right?" Hunter slyly placed the blame back on Amber. It was what he was skillful at doing.

A faint flush of guilt coloured Amber's cheeks. "Yes, I do," she said, flicking her eyes from him to the window.

The lowering slant of the afternoon sun indicated the approaching evening. Leaves in the tree canopies swayed with the soft breeze blowing. Amber saw Lily in the yard, her eyes lit with laughter, as she chased after Bessie, and Madison chased after both. Unexpectedly, Amber felt the tug of jealousy press down on her chest—again— but Hunter couldn't know how deeply the disappointment cut into her heart, and she tamped her emotions.

"If you've set your mind on Madison to be Lily's nanny, I'm on board," Hunter said.

Amber wasn't set on anything. She didn't want Madison in Lily's life, and seeing the look Madison and Hunter exchanged, she regretted letting her into their home and life. Until Amber figured out what to do with Madison, what choice did she have?

Amber said, "Thank you."

Chapter 11

FROM THE KITCHEN window, Amber watched Madison and Lily jump into the pool for Lily's swimming lessons. With the days becoming warmer as spring slid into summer, it was yet another activity of the many Madison slated for Lily in the past few weeks. Madison had Lily playing baseball and sailing on the lake, and she was teaching her how to bake cookies and muffins. All activities Lily appeared to enjoy, which Amber never thought to ask her daughter if she was interested in doing, let alone doing with her.

Madison pulled Lily out of the ballet, violin, and French lessons Amber had enrolled her in. Lily hated the classes and was doing them to please her mother.

"She's five years old, Amber fun is what she wants to do," Madison told Amber. "If Lily's to become a violinist or a ballet dancer, she will ask for the training. You can't force someone to do what they don't want to or turn them into what they're not."

It never occurred to Amber that Lily didn't enjoy the classes, and she hated Madison for having the foresight to see what she couldn't.

Amber could kick herself for not asking Lily if she was enjoying herself. Amber assumed Lily did as much as she eventually had when her mother enrolled her in similar classes to shape and mould her into a refined young lady.

Amber might not have thought to ask Lily about her likes and dislikes. She might not be spending as much time as she should with Lily. Amber might not be able to go swimming, boating, or spend time at the playground with Lily, but she was a working mother. Amber told herself to ease her guilt. She was the family's breadwinner, and there were only twenty-four hours in the day.

Still, resentment and fear washed over Amber. She resented Madison for knowing her child better than she did and feared her for having the motherly instincts she lacked.

Madison was claiming her place in Lily's life.

What was Amber to do? Did she quit the job she loved? A job she'd worked hard for and sacrificed all to attain. Amber was at the top of her game. Tell Me All was the number one rated afternoon talk show with national exposure. Syndication of the show to the United States and Europe was in the works.

It wasn't the money or the recognition Amber prized. Amber valued the sense of accomplishment and confidence she came away with after every successful show.

Amber wasn't a good wife. If she were, Hunter wouldn't have sought comfort in the arms of another woman. And Madison made it clear she wasn't a good mother.

Amber loved Lily, but she also prized her job. What was Amber to do?

Hunter walked up and stood next to Amber at the window. "You were right."

"About?"

"Madison. She's good with our Lily." Hunter took a sip from the coffee cup in his hand.

"Yes, she is." Amber watched Madison in the pool buoy, Lily, with her arms as she showed her how to float with her face in the water.

"And Lily seems to like her very much." Hunter's eyes were fixed on Madison, and her golden skin against the pure white of her bikini was titillating.

As much as she could feel the resentment burn her chest like battery acid, Amber swallowed the irksomeness and said, "Yes, she does. I got to get to work." She turned to walk out of the kitchen and caught the intense flare of desire in Hunter's eyes. Amber looked at Hunter hard for a long minute. "Shouldn't you be getting to work also?" she snapped.

Hunter glanced at Amber's heated face. "What's that look for?"

Her temper flared. "Mine? You should see yours," she said, flicking her eyes from him to Madison.

"Christ, Amber, there are times you're exhausting." He dropped the coffee mug on the counter. "Whatever's going through that tiny brain of yours, stop it. Now."

"I'm sorry, baby. I didn't think. I didn't mean what I said." Amber's voice was rusty and unsteady.

"You meant every word. That you think I'd be interested in Madison, a child, is bad, but the grovelling, Amber, is pathetic." Hunter stormed out of the room.

Chapter 12

RIBBONS OF LIGHT from the sun-washed summer sky smiled on the city and came through the guesthouse windows to light the room bright. The home smelled of the shortbread cookies baking in the oven. Lily knelt on a bar stool at the kitchen island and stirred batter in the bowl. Her pigtails bounced with the motion.

Lily stopped stirring to allow Madison to add two tablespoons of vanilla to the mixture. Flour dusted her forehead and cheek face. "I've never made shortbread cookies before." Lily had on a yellow romper with a frilly shirt.

"Neither have I. So, this is what you call experimenting, but I think we're okay. We have all the ingredients, and I followed the recipe to the letter." Madison shut down the laptop. "Let's hope they come out tasting good as Mama Cookie Maker claims they will." Today Madison wore tight jeans and an orange T-shirt with a square front pocket. Her hair was shoulder-length, and on her feet were sandals.

"Who's Mama Cookie?" Lily asked.

"Some wanna-be celebrity seizing her fifteen minutes of fame online."

"Huh?"

"Never mind, peanut."

"Well, if they don't come out good, we can try again. I like baking with you, Madison. I like doing a lot of things with you."

Madison lifted a hand and ran it over Lily's hair. "Me, too, peanut."

Six weeks working as Lily's nanny, the pint-size girl had claimed Madison's heart lock, stock, and barrel. Lily filled Madison's life with a beautiful peace she'd never known, with the love she'd never felt. For the first time in her life, Madison's heart spilled with love that knew no bounds.

Madison did nothing extraordinary with Lily. Madison played with her, took her for walks by the lake, and watched over her when she played at the park. They swam in the pool and ate peanut butter and strawberry jelly sandwiches—Lily's favourite. Madison gave Lily combed her hair into the pigtails she liked after her bath. Ordinary tasks that felt extraordinary because of Lily, something Madison hadn't had in her life with her mother.

"It looks as if Bessie can't wait to eat the cookies," Madison said when the dog plopped down on her rump, eyes peeled on the oven door.

"Mommy says she's like a chomking machine."

"I think you mean chomping, peanut."

"Yeah, that's it.

"And she'd be right. Bessie does love to eat."

"Who doesn't?" said the woman at the front door.

With cagey eyes, the women stared at one another.

The woman wore a white tapered suit with black piping that clung to long, slender curves and set off the long red hair that flowed in waves around her face down to her shoulders. The red Louboutin slingbacks at her feet matched the tote that hung from her arm. Her freshly manicured nails, painted cherry-red, matched her lipstick. She was the epitome of glamour and style.

"Auntie Sam." Lily stood on the chair and wiggled her hands, summoning Sam into a hug.

Madison dug into her memory and didn't remember the private investigator's report mentioning Amber had a sister.

"Hello, my favourite girl." Sam embraced Lily tightly while studying Madison with a lawyerly eye over her shoulder. "And who might you be?"

"This is Madison, Auntie Sam. She's my nanny," Lily said. "This is Auntie Sam, and she's mom's bestest friend in the whole world."

"So you're the great nanny I've heard much about from Lily."

"She is, Auntie Sam. Madison plays with me and takes me to the park. I made a lot of friends there. Sometimes we go swimming, and sometimes we bake. Like today, we're making cookies. I helped make them. You smell them." Lily breathed in their scent and rambled on for another ten minutes giving a detailed account of her baking experience.

The joy in the child's voice had Sam wondering how Madison had survived Amber's jealousy. It wasn't like Amber to stand by and allow another woman to muscle into her territory. Something didn't smell right.

"You, my love, have the gift of the gab and need to consider a career in law." Sam helped Lily off the chair when she opened her arms to be lifted. "Anyone who makes my Lily happy is okay in my books. It's nice to meet you, Madison." Sam stepped forward, hand extended.

Madison took Sam's hand and pumped it. "Nice to meet you, Auntie Sam."

Lily's lips stretched out in a smile. "She's not your auntie, silly."

"You are so right, my love. Do I look that old? Sam will do, Madison." Sam put her handbag on the counter. "It does smell great in here."

"It's the shortbread cookies baking in the oven," Lily said.

Sam said, "Your favourite."

"And Bessie's," Lily added when the dog barked. "She's been watching them cook this whole time." Lily looked up at Sam and signalled her to come closer. When Sam leaned down to Lily, she whispered, "Did you bring me a present?"

Sam reached into her tote for the bag containing a tub of ice cream. "It's chocolate ice cream."

Lily shrieked, "My other favourite food and yours."

"That's right, and you know what chocolate ice cream goes great with? Hot shortbread cookies."

"Which we'll have in twenty-five minutes," Madison said, looking at the stove's timer and taking Sam's ice cream tub. "Hopefully. It's my first time baking shortbread cookies."

"It's better than I can do. I don't even know how to turn the oven on." Sam's comment elicited a snorting laugh from Lily.

"Can I go outside to play with Bessie?" Lily asked.

"Fine, but don't go far." Both women said in unison, mirroring their winged brows.

"I won't. Come on, Bessie. Let's go outside." Lily ran out of the house, and Bessie raced forward with her tongue lolling.

Sam watched Madison put the ice cream in the freezer. "She's happier than I've ever seen her. Don't get me wrong, Amber and Hunter love her to death, but they lead busy lives and don't spend as much time as they should with that little girl." Sam walked to the living room and caught sight of the mail on the coffee table. The envelopes addressed to Madison were to a P.O. Box address. Post office boxes were for people running from something or hiding from someone. Sam wondered which it was for Madison. "It's one of the reasons I choose not to have children. Either you're all in, or you're not. I'm too selfish to be all in."

"I guess it's the cost of success." Madison could hear Lily's laughter and Bessie's bark from the front yard.

Sam sat on the sofa lined with teal and brown pillows. "That sounds like a Hunter quote."

Madison's brow lift was the only movement she made to convey her reply.

Sam smirked. "I thought so. I bet you he has you calling him Mr. Roche."

Madison's brow remained high above impassive eyes.

Sam met Madison's eye. "I'm a stranger to you and Amber's dear friend, but you don't have to hide your disdain for Mr. Roche from me. I'm not a fan, and Amber knows it well."

As glad as Madison was to hear Sam wasn't a supporter of Hunter's, she didn't know Sam well enough to enter into girl talk. You never knew when you were being played.

"Can I get you a cup of coffee, Sam? I have a nifty new espresso machine, compliments of Amber. She's generous that way."

Another moocher, living off Amber. "What I'd like is a martini with two olives. I've had a hell of a morning, but I'll take the coffee. Can that thing make cappuccino?"

"It can." Madison turned the coffee maker on.

"Then that's what I'll have with two sweeteners." Sam crossed one slender leg over another.

"Coming right up." Madison poured coffee beans into the grinder. "You're a lawyer, Sam."

"I am. Am I so predictable?"

"It's what you suggested Lily consider as a career," Madison added the ground coffee into the portafilter and tamped it. "Most of us suggest the career that is us."

"Observant and profound." Sam watched Madison attach the portafilter to the head of the espresso machine, and seconds later, coffee poured into a cappuccino cup. Its aroma mingled with the baking shortbread. Next, Madison seamlessly moved to pour milk into a small pitcher that she placed underneath the steam wand. The milk began to froth. "You sure know your way around that machine."

"I was a barista or, as we called it in the trade, a poor person's psychologist. Dealing with the public, you get to learn how to read people." Madison turned an eye out the door when Bessie's barks got louder from the front yard as Lily encouraged the dog to fetch the stick she threw.

"Tip for you. Don't let Amber catch you letting Lily out on her own like that. She would freak out."

"Thanks for the head up, but I always have her in my sight. Besides, she's a good girl and does what she's told." Madison poured frothy milk onto the coffee in the cup.

"You and I know that, but Amber's the essence of a helicopter parent. Sometimes she loves that girl too much."

"It sounds as if you don't agree with helicopter parenting." Madison poured frothy milk into a second cup.

"Is that skim milk?" Sam asked, and Madison shook her head.

"Sorry, I only have whole milk because of Lily. Besides, no decent cappuccino is made with skim milk?"

"Guess I'll have to pass up on the chocolate ice cream. These hips can't afford it."

"Cinnamon?" Madison waved the shaker at Sam. "It's calorie-free."

Sam smiled. "Pour it on, back to your parenting question. I'm more of an autonomous type and can't stand my every move monitored. It's why I run my firm my way and will forever be single. Don't get me wrong. I like the company of men, but in limited doses and mainly for sex."

"Respect." Madison handed Sam the cappuccino.

"Do you have a man in your life, Madison?"

Madison took the chair across from Sam. "Don't need one. They're like a giant boil on the ass, and I've found them not to be good in bed."

With a slow curving lip, Sam lifted her cup in salute. "We're going to get along just fine, Madison."

Madison gave Sam a slow, intimate survey over the rim of her cappuccino cup. "What type of lawyer are you?"

"Criminal. Are you in need of my services?" Sam joked.

Madison reached into her jeans pocket and pulled out a one-dollar bill. "Take it."

Sam took the money. Then it hit her, and she sat up straight. "You're not a criminal, are you? Not that I mind. Criminals keep my bank account flush, but if you lean toward criminality, I don't want you around, Lily."

"No, I'm not a criminal. I want some advice, and if you're my lawyer, anything I discuss with you becomes solicitor-client privileged, right? You can't tell anyone what we discuss, not even Amber."

"That's right." Intrigued, Sam eyed Madison as she sank back into the depths of the sofa. "What is it you wish to discuss?"

"I need to know.... First, let's start with this." Madison reached for the locket around her neck and clicked it open. Pinching the heart-shaped photograph inside it, she handed it to Sam.

Sam studied the photograph of the blonde woman with large smiling eyes. "She's beautiful. Who is she?"

"I have no idea. She came with the locket."

Sam's brow furrowed, and confusion filled her eyes. "I don't understand."

"It's not the photograph I want you to look at, but what's on the back."

Sam set her cup on the coffee table, picked the photograph from the locket, and flipped it. "What is it?" she said, studying the sequence of numbers.

Madison shrugged her shoulders. "A P.I.N. number, a bank account number, I don't know. It's what I need you to find out for me."

"Who do they belong to?"

"I'm not sure."

Sam met Madison's eyes. "Why do you have this?"

"I can't tell you until you find out what they are, and for transparency's sake, I have limited funds, like in almost none."

Sam leaned back in her seat and gave a quick shake of her head. "So, let me get this straight. You, a stranger to me, want me to spend time and money tracking a random sequence of numbers that you have no idea what it is or if it'll lead anywhere. You refuse to tell me why and have no money to back this venture up."

Madison levelled a serious look at Sam's apprehensive face. "Yes, that's correct. So, will you do it?"

"As tempting as it sounds…."

Madison stopped Sam. "I guarantee if you find out what those numbers pertain to and connect them to their owner, it will be worth your while."

Sam drummed her fingers on the sofa's arm while debating her response. Sam had to admit the woman sitting across from her intrigued and challenged her curiosity.

"Okay, I'll help you, but only because I enjoy a good mystery. I'll get my private investigator on it. She's the best, but keep in mind we have little to go on."

Madison's eyes glinted with satisfaction. "Thank you."

The oven timer went off, and Lily came running through the front door with Bessie sprinting after her.

"The cookies I made are ready. The cookies I made are ready, Bessie." The excitement in her voice was intoxicating, and Bessie set off in zoomies around the house.

"Yes, they are, peanut." Madison rose and slanted a look over her shoulder at Sam. "Remember, not a word to Amber about this."

Sam made the universal symbol of turning the key in her pursed mouth while wondering what rabbit hole this led to.

Part II

The Middle

We are our actions.

—M.L. Lexi

Chapter 13

MADISON RAISED THE volume on the television when
Amber appeared on the screen. Amber looked stylish in a
beige belted jacket with large pearl buttons and slim
ankle-high cigarette pants. Her hair was twisted in a bun;
wisps fountained around her face. She looked star-like,
beautiful and poised.

The camera zoomed back for a long shot of Amber
and her guest, a woman whose husband had cheated with
her best friend. Natasha, a blond, middle-aged woman,
twenty-five pounds overweight, with the roadmap of her
miserable life tracked on her pale face, told all. Amber
listened closely as Natasha spilled her guts on national
television about her pathetic, cheating husband.

"The bastard slept with that slut in our home, in our
bed. It's where I found them when I came home early
from work. They weren't expecting me." Anger audibly
roiled up in the studio audience composed mainly of
women. The sisterhood hissed, cursed, and offered
Natasha words of sympathy.

The camera zoomed in on Natasha and stayed focused
on her as she wiped her tears with the tissue Amber
handed her. "Imagine the shock of not only finding him in
bed with another woman, but that woman being your
childhood friend."

"No, I can't imagine. I'm so sorry you had to experience that, Natasha," Amber said, her face radiating sympathy. "How betrayed you must have felt?"

The camera did a quick pan of the audience when many shook their heads in anger and disgust at the betrayal, and others turned to their neighbour to express their thoughts.

"Angry, hurt, and rejected was how I felt," the indignant Natasha said while Madison set chicken and diced carrots into the pan and sprinkled olive oil per the recipe.

Madison set the pan in the oven at three-hundred-and-fifty and the timer for one hour. Madison then added diced potatoes to the boiling water on the stove for the mashed potato she planned to serve with the chicken for dinner. Lily was an adventurous eater, and Madison made as many foods as her limited cooking skills allowed.

"Then I find out he's been taking money from our joint accounts. Money which I worked hard for to support his extracurricular activities with that slut." Natasha air-quoted extracurricular.

"Did you not know he was skimming your bank accounts?"

Madison thought the question from Amber was more a statement than a question. It was only that morning that Madison heard Amber and Hunter arguing about money as she walked past their bedroom on her way to get Lily to get her ready for school. Far be it for Madison to pass up an opportunity to eavesdrop, and she stopped outside the bedroom door to listen.

"Just asking, baby, but I noticed you wrote a cheque from our joint account to a linen supplier for five thousand dollars." Amber's tone was subdued.

"I did. I told you about having to pay a linen supplier. Don't you remember?" Hunter said, rummaging through the drawer for a pair of socks.

"I do, but five thousand for linen?"

"It's more than just linen. It's uniforms and aprons and everything linen." When the silence lingered, Hunter straightened from his hunch as he slid on his socks to look Amber in the eyes. "I see the doubt in your face. Do you not believe me, baby?"

There was a fifteen-second pause before Amber said, "I do, baby. I do, but…." There was a longer pause now. "I just wish we could save more money for Lily's education and future." It was the best counter Amber could offer on the spot.

"And we will."

"But that restaurant seems to be draining much of our income." Amber made it the collective our for Hunter's benefit because the household income was solely her contribution.

Hunter had never been good at managing money. He'd drawn more than contributed to their bank account in their ten-year marriage.

"You know the restaurant business is a fickle one." Because Amber's face creased into deeper doubtful lines, Hunter pulled her into his arms and held her tight. "Baby, you know everything I do is for you, Lily, for our family. All this will pay off soon enough. With your help, I'm almost there. We're a team, aren't we?"

"We are that but…."

"Let's not waste time with idle chat."

Through the door, Madison heard kissing noises she perceived initiated by Hunter to silence Amber and derail the conversation that didn't benefit him.

Soft moans and groans followed from Amber. Resentment tightened Madison's belly. Hunter didn't love Amber. Madison heard it in his voice and saw it in his eyes. Hunter deserved more, and Madison would see he got it.

Madison's mind racing and plotting, she turned toward Lily's bedroom.

"What did you do when you discovered the missing money?" Amber asked Natasha, stirring a dose of amplified compassion into the question.

The camera zoomed in on Natasha's face to capture her projected emotion. "I threw his cheating ass out of the house, changed all the passwords on our bank accounts and had my lawyer freeze access to the investment accounts," Natasha said triumphantly.

Applause and cheers of support and approval for Natasha from the audience followed.

Madison thought there was no more remarkable anger than that of a woman scorned as she added a peeled garlic clove and a sprinkle of salt to the boiling potatoes.

Chapter 14

AMBER'S FRIDAY NIGHT appearance at Hunter's Carpaccio Ristorante came with the fanfare a celebrity commanded. It came with the spotlight, diners' attention, their need to rub elbows with a known star, and the publicity. And all was a deliberately staged performance by Hunter to boost his restaurant's profile and profitability.

And it always paid off. The restaurant was swamped with the Friday night crowd. The stools at the bar were filled with drinking patrons with refined palates flashing their credit cards. By night's end, those cards would be charged thousands of dollars.

Hunter's five-star rated restaurant was elegant and modern. Chocolate-brown floors, brass, and ebony gleamed. Salmon-coloured linen and bright, expensive Italian splashy art hung on walls made to look like brickwork complemented the decor. A three-month wait list for a reservation was partly due to the bi-monthly cooking appearances Amber coerced her producer to schedule on her show for Hunter.

The first time Hunter appeared on Tell Me All, he did nothing more than make a tasty vinaigrette. Hunter's innocuous appearance resulted in increased ratings. Hunter's pretty face and smouldering sexuality were what Amber's daytime female viewers guzzled along with their boxed wine.

Soon enough, the emails from ardent viewers poured in for Hunter. Some emails praised Hunter's cooking skills. Other emails thanked him for sharing his techniques and for what they learned. Many viewers complimented the unique recipes he offered on the show. Most, however, were graphic, from women asking Hunter for one-on-one cooking lessons any place, anytime. Hunter kept those emails from Amber.

Amber couldn't understand why Hunter claimed the restaurant was bleeding money and how with all of his success, he continued to dip into their joint account. Why Hunter put subsidizing the restaurant above saving for Lily's education and future was a question Amber often asked herself.

There have been many arguments about it, but the result was always the same. Amber pointed out the restaurant was draining their savings, and Hunter wriggled out by reminding her his contribution to her show—for which he received no money—was what got her the million-dollar paycheque. Amber couldn't contest the remark, and they'd circle back to how it was.

All eyes turned to Hunter when he stepped out of the kitchen to greet Amber with diners looking on—all part of the Friday night act. Hunter had been in the kitchen for the past few hours, yet he looked like he'd stepped off a photo shoot. His hair and fashionable stubble were a bouncy dark contrast to the pristine white chef coat.

Hunter aimed his glacial blue eyes and a wide smile at Amber. With the pleasure of knowing it was for her and he was her man came an equal amount of jealousy when every woman in the room eyed him like a prime piece of wagyu steak.

"Hey, honey." Hunter brushed his lips to Amber's sweetly and tenderly and washed away all Amber's fears. "You can bring them in. Full house again tonight."

Amber wore white silk with white pumps and pearls at her neck. "Glad to be of service."

Hunter's face went brilliant with pleasure as he looked around at the full tables. "We should rake it in tonight," he whispered in her ear.

"Hi, Daddy. I'm wearing a new dress." Lily twirled to make her purple tulip dress puffed out.

"Hi, baby." Hunter kissed Lily's forehead. "And don't you look beautiful?"

"Thank you. Madison helped me pick my dress. She said it was the perfect dress for our dinner tonight."

Hunter stole a glance at Madison. "And she'd be right." His expression was a mixture of surprise and approval.

The short yellow dress with a thigh-high slit painted over her curvy body that replaced Madison's usual jeans and T-shirt looked better on her than it had on Amber. The same went for the yellow slingbacks that never made Amber's legs look as long as Madison's. Madison's long hair, shiny and silky, fell in waves around a subtly painted face.

Madison cleaned up nicely, and Hunter stared at her a moment longer before turning to Sam. "And look who flew in on her broom to mooch a free meal," Hunter said, turning to Sam.

Sam looked stylish in the brown Carolina Herrera boat-neck jacket and the knee-high pencil skirt. "I have celebrity power too, Hunter. If you haven't been keeping up, I'm all over the news as the lawyer who reinstated Mrs. Feldman's parental rights to the children, her husband, Ari Feldman, CEO of the Feldman Media Empire, sequestered."

The middle-aged, blonde woman behind Sam, waiting for her table, jumped into the conversation. "You stick it to them, sister. That bastard got what he deserved," she said with some flourish before the maître d led her away.

"A supporter of your feminist slaughter," Hunter said.

Sam gave Hunter a smug smile. "Chopping off tiny testicles is what I live for."

"I'd say more devouring than chop is what you do best," Hunter commented.

"Behave, children," Amber murmured. "We're here to have a meal and enjoy ourselves."

"Yes, we are. Show us to our table, garçon." Sam stepped aside for Hunter to lead the way.

The woman could rile him, and Hunter took a deep calming breath. "I have the usual table reserved for my two favourite ladies."

"Aww, I'm touched." Sam's mouth tipped up at the corners.

Yes, the woman always managed to get under his skin.

Throughout the Caesar salad, gnocchi, chicken Marsala meal, and pizza for Lily, a parade of Amber's fans waved or stopped by the table to ask for selfies. Obligingly, Amber smiled and posed for every request. Some patrons even asked Sam to pose with them.

Although Madison remained in the shadows, she drank in the spectacle and loved every moment. The swanky surroundings and the five-star-rated meal ranked high compared to the coffee and muffins Madison was used to eating on the run.

Fun was better, and rich was incontestably better.

Madison was having the time of her life. This was Madison's scene and where she belonged. Madison determined to do everything she could to squeeze all she could from Amber to remain in her new life.

Chapter 15

THE CLOCK READ 1:00 a.m. when Hunter got home from the restaurant. Amber had gone to bed shortly after getting home at eleven. Lily, who fell asleep on the car ride home with the excitement of the dinner at her father's restaurant, was tucked away in her bed.

Madison was doing laps in the swimming pool. She enjoyed the late-night swims when the world was quiet and almost dreamlike. A full moon sailed high in the sky, and its light misted the land and the lake in a blue haze. The air was ripe with the rich scents of earth and summer. Cicadas and frogs sang to their mates. From somewhere, a dog barked, and another barked back in response. The pleasant smell of lilac and the sweetness of roses mingled with the pool's chlorinated water.

The movement in the pool water gleaming with underwater lights caught Hunter's attention as he walked to the kitchen refrigerator. Hunter grabbed two beer bottles when he spotted Madison and walked to the pool's edge. Pushing her towel aside, Hunter sat on the lounge chair, drank beer, and watched Madison with keen eyes.

Stroke after powerful stroke, her long, slim body glided through the water with a swimmer's fluidity. When she reached the end of the pool, she dove in, pushed off the tiled wall, and swam toward the opposite end. She did that ten more times before she swam to the pool's edge.

"You're a strong swimmer," Hunter said when she leaned her forearms on the pool's edge to lift herself out of the water.

"I didn't know anyone was here." Madison brushed shiny, wet, dark hair from her face. "I usually swim late at night, not to disturb anyone."

"I'm glad someone does. We rarely use the pool, and swimming is what it's there for." Hunter's eyes never left Madison. In the white bikini that accentuated the bronze skin and curves glistening with water, she looked too tasty for Hunter to look away.

Feeling his hungry eyes on her, understanding what was going through his head, Madison bent over to reach for the towel on the lounge chair to give him a clear view of her assets.

"I got you a beer." Hunter held the bottle out to Madison.

"You read my mind." Madison's lips curved in a sultry smile.

"Did you enjoy yourself tonight at the restaurant?" Hunter watched Madison spread the towel on the lounge chair.

"I did." Madison rounded her lips and wrapped them on the bottleneck to take an indulgent drink. The performance put a pleasant hum in Hunter's blood. "The food was as good as I remember. You're an excellent chef, Hunter."

"Thank you." Hunter tossed some of his beer back. "It's too bad things didn't work out then."

"It is."

Flashes of memory to the time Madison worked for Hunter came to her.

Madison was fifteen and took the first job offered at her mother's insistence she carried her weight at home. Hunter was tall, handsome, and generous to a naïve, inexperienced, desperate girl. On the spot, Hunter offered Madison the waitressing job above the hourly rate, and Madison jumped at the chance.

Hunter took the time to train her and answer all her questions. None of that helped. Madison still turned out to be a lousy server, unable to deal with the public or bend to the retail mantra the customer was always right.

Madison's time at Carpaccio Ristorante was a short six months, but the memories would last a lifetime.

"I've never been good at dealing with demanding, unreasonable people who only want things their way." Madison sipped her beer slowly, contemplatively.

"I remember. You were a fiery one, a lousy server, but a loaded pistol nonetheless. You kept things interesting. It's why I kept you on."

"I know." She leaned back on her elbows, stretched the long legs that never seemed to end out and got his attention as she meant to do.

The hunger for Madison speared into Hunter hot and sharp. It had been so long since Hunter felt a good jolt to the groin. Hunter took a moment. "I never thanked you for everything you did for me. We left on bad terms, and I apologize for that."

"You're so sweet, but there's no need for apologies. Let bygones be bygones. That's what I always say." Madison drank more beer.

"Good. Me too." Hunter took a swig of beer. "It feels as if fate had you end up here, in my home."

"How do you know it's fate?"

Hunter cocked an eyebrow. "Did you purposely end up here because of me?"

Propping herself on her elbow, Madison turned to face him. Her ripe breasts spilled over the edge of her bikini bra. It pleased her to see the rabid look that came over his eyes. "You could say that."

"Well, I'm glad you're here." Hunter's voice hitched. Christ, she made things explode inside him. He found it difficult to grind down the want rising in him. "I couldn't say anything earlier in front of Amber and Sam, but you looked great tonight. You look … really great now." Hunter's pulse raced and pounded in hard, greedy waves.

"Thank you." She gave him a clear, direct look as she skimmed fingers across the long line of her thigh up to her breast.

Hunter felt himself go hard, but acting on it with Amber upstairs wasn't possible then. He looked up in the direction of their bedroom window. The blinds were drawn closed, and no lights glowed. If Amber saw Hunter talking to Madison, her mind would go into crazy mode, and her jealousy would dial to a unreasoningly level. Amber would get rid of Madison, and Hunter's plan for her would become moot. The itch Hunter needed to be scratched by Madison wouldn't be satisfied.

"I want to be with you," Hunter said as easily as ordering dessert.

Madison's grin spread wide. "Me too," she said, and Hunter let out an unsteady breath.

"Why don't you come by the restaurant tomorrow night? I could knock off early, and we can watch the evening settle from my downtown apartment."

With a smile ripe with sexual innuendo, Madison pushed off the lounge chair to her feet. "That sounds like a great plan, but how about I meet you at the apartment? I don't want eyes on me at the restaurant. Some of your staff recognized me at dinner."

Intelligent, beautiful, sexy, and cunning, Madison was his kind of woman. "Yes, that's a much better idea. "No need to set off the murmurs or be looking over our shoulders," he said, rattling off the address.

Madison leaned over and, in his ear, whispered, "I only have good ideas. I'll show you some tomorrow night." Her eyes sparkle with mischief.

Cruising on anticipatory bliss, he went harder. "I can't wait."

Madison reached down with her hand to stroke his rock-hard penis. "Seems he can't either." Her touch filled his veins with fire.

Hunter's attention drifted for a moment to lustful thoughts. "No. No, he can't. I want you now."

"Patience is a virtue." She reached for the towel on the chair and walked away.

Watching her sway her tight, round butt, Hunter swallowed hard.

AMBER WATCHED THE SCENE BETWEEN MADISON and Hunter, playing out from the darkness of her bedroom window. Amber saw Madison splay her wet body in that skimpy bikini across the chaise lounge to lure and seduce Hunter.

Contrary to popular belief, men, not women, were the weaker sex and women, not men, controlled the tide of life—through sex. Given a rush of forbidden anticipation, weakened a man and reduced him to a submissive puppet. Intelligent women like Madison knew it and knew how to exploit a man's weakness to further her interests.

Women were deceitful, manipulative bitches who flaunted their sexuality to control the narrative and gain power over the man they set their sights on. Madison was no exception as she made a play for her husband, in her home, under her nose.

Eyes blazing with pure rage, Amber watched Madison rest her hands on the hard plane of her husband's chest and lean in to whisper in his ear. Amber wished she knew what Madison was saying to bait Hunter into her web.

The pressure in Amber's chest knotted tight when she watched the lustful look in Hunter's eyes and a satisfied Madison walk away with a brimming smile.

The woman she allowed into her home was taking over every aspect of her life. Madison was taking over her house, claiming her daughter as her own, and now, she was after her husband.

And there was nothing Amber could do about it.

Any move she made against Madison risked her going public with what she knew. Amber would lose everything and everyone in her life and end up behind bars for a long time.

Feeling defeated, Amber stared after Madison as she returned to her guesthouse.

Chapter 16

AMBER STEPPED INTO the kitchen to the smell of brewing coffee, frying eggs, bacon, and baking. The television on the counter was tuned to the local weather station. The busty woman with the low V-neck sweater standing before a map of the city claimed today would be a hot and sunny June day.

Lily sat at the table. A glass of milk, a plate of scrambled eggs, a slice of bacon, and a piece of buttered toast sat in front of her. She wore a lime-green jumper over a white T-shirt and glowing Barbie sandals. Her pigtails were tied with the orange satin ribbons she picked out.

Bessie plopped down on her rump at Lily's feet and looked up at Lily with hopeful eyes waiting for bacon scraps.

"Good morning, pumpkin." Amber kissed the top of Lily's head. Amber wore jeans, a flowing teal blouse, and sandals displaying manicured toenails.

"Good morning, Mommy. Me and Madison made muffins."

"Madison and I made muffins," Amber corrected.

"Yeah. They're in the oven cooking." Lily breathed in the scent. "Do you smell them, Mommy?"

"I do. They smell delicious." Amber picked up a mug and poured coffee. "You're becoming a regular Betty Crocker."

"That's what Madison says?" Lily washed down buttered toast with milk.

"She did, did she?" Amber's face went tight when resentment and anger pushed straight to her belly, tightening it.

It irritated Amber to feel the jealousy stir in her as strongly as it did, and helpless she could not push it away. Madison was claiming her daughter as her own and sidling to her husband.

Amber had no one but herself to blame.

Amber never thought to bake with Lily, and she had never made the time to go for long walks or take her to the playground as Madison did. Amber made little time for Hunter, but goddammit, she was the breadwinner. She had a taxing job that demanded all her energy and time. Sacrifices had to be made to provide the comfortable lifestyle they enjoyed, the beautiful home they lived in, and financially back the restaurant.

Or so Amberggh told herself to appease her guilt.

It was the cost of success. Family or career was the choice, especially for a woman. It was an or, not an and, for women as it was for men. No matter what feminists said, women couldn't do it all.

Amber took a calming breath to tone down her racing mind.

"This little lady has some baking skills." Madison set down the plate of fruit salad in front of Amber when she sat at the kitchen table. "You look tired, Amber. Didn't you sleep well?"

"I'm fine," Amber said between clenched teeth. "I want eggs and bacon with toast this morning."

"Mommy, you always said bacon is too fat for your body."

Madison's eyes puzzled. "What she said."

"I know what I want, and I want bacon, eggs, and toast this morning. Let me have the damn eggs." Amber snapped and immediately regretted it when Lily looked at her with owl-round eyes. "Please," Amber added, biting back the urge to question Madison about her conversation with Hunter last night for Lily's benefit.

"Coming right up." Madison plated the food and brought it to Amber.

Madison looked overdressed in maroon leggings, a white tank top, and running shoes compared to last night, Amber thought.

"Lily, I've decided not to go into the office today. How about you and me spend the day together."

"It's you and I, Mommy." Bessie's patience paid off when Lily tossed her a strip of bacon. "Madison and I were going to the mall today. There's a carnimal there."

Amber's eyes went flat. Madison, Madison, Madison was all she heard from Lily lately, and she was getting sick and tired of it.

"It's carnival, peanut." Madison topped Amber's coffee.

"They have a merry-go-round, and Madison said there'll be animals I can pet. I want to pet the animals, and you don't like animals, Mommy. Bessie's the only animal you like. You said so." Bessie lifted her head out of her water bowl and barked.

"Mommy doesn't have to pet the animals. You will," Madison said. "You'll have lots of fun with your mother."

"Okay," Lily said with a pout.

"It's a date, pumpkin," Amber said, biting back the injured feeling that assailed her at the idea Lily had to be coerced into spending time with her. "If you're finished with breakfast, brush your teeth and wash your hands. You can watch television in your room until we leave in an hour when the mall opens. I'm looking forward to our day together, baby."

"Me too, Mommy. Can Bessie come with us?"

"Of course, she can." Amber's reply came swiftly to preclude Madison from answering on her behalf.

"You hear that, Bessie. You're coming with us." The dog barked her acknowledgement with a smile. "Come on, Bessie, let's go brush my teeth."

Amber cocked her head and swept a pleased look at Madison when Lily merrily walked out of the kitchen with Bessie in tow. "I hope this didn't interfere with your plans."

Madison picked up Lily's plate and glass and wiped the table clean. "This works out perfectly. I have an appointment I'd like to get to today, and I was debating how to do it with Lily."

Amber felt the tension skitter along her neck and bunch in the muscles around her shoulders. "Doing anything special?"

"Not really. I'm just meeting a friend. I won't be long. An hour or so is all I need, and I'll be home before you."

Madison was meeting Hunter. Amber felt it in her bones. It was what the conversation between Madison and Hunter by the pool last night was about, and she helped facilitate it.

Madison was one step closer to stealing her husband, and Amber could do nothing about it.

Chapter 17

IN HER OFFICE, Sam pushed off from behind the oak desk and walked to the sideboard. Reaching into the mini-refrigerator, she drew a bottle of water. Behind Sam, the large windows of her corner office gave a view of the blue sky, the calm lake, and the busy city below.

Sam believed art filled the soul with the calm and joy her job sometimes robbed from her. A Jackson Pollock, dripping with colour, hung on the wall facing her desk. Mayan stonework, blown Murano glasswork, and Italian and German paintings hung on walls throughout the office floor for her staff to appreciate and enjoy.

Sam was as demanding of her staff as she was generous with her money. Sam's philosophy and that which she instilled in her staff were that financial and personal rewards came with hard work. The financial reward derived from that hard work was meant to be shared with her team, primarily women who wouldn't otherwise be encouraged to excel under male management. But it had to be earned.

True to her word, Sam had made those who worked hard and built a reputation for themselves and the firm very wealthy.

Today, Sam was a vision of grace and understatement in a lavender Armani pantsuit with a cream silk blouse. The four-inch Jimmy Choo pumps at her feet matched the colour of her blouse.

Sam waved in her private investigator when she knocked on the glass door. No one would guess Lisa was a private investigator. She was thin but fit with a youthful, pretty face. Lisa looked younger than her thirty years in khaki pants and a moss-green hoodie with the words Girl Power printed across her chest. Her blond ponytail was threaded through the opening of the Blue Jays baseball cap.

"So, what did you find out about Madison Donnell?" Sam waved Lisa to a guest chair, and she sat at the high back chair behind her desk.

"The post office box registered under Madison Donnell is located downtown."

"Miles away from where she lives now." Sam pointed out.

"Yeah, that's what I thought, but it could be because she recently moved to your friend's place and hasn't had time to transfer it closer." Lisa blew blond bangs out of her eyes. "All the mail she gets there is forwarded junk mail and bills, nothing of interest or out of the ordinary."

Sam's eyebrows lift in mild surprise. "You got access to the box's contents. How?"

Lisa stretched back in the chair and crossed her legs at the ankles. "Do you really want to know?"

Sam shook her head. "You're right. I don't. Where is it being forwarded from?"

"This is where it gets interesting." Lisa rested her folded hands on her flat belly. "It's forwarded from her mother's place. And yes, the question is, why? Why would Madison tell her mother to mail her to a post office box and not directly to her current residence address?"

"That doesn't sound all that cagey." Sam sipped at her water. "Grab yourself a bottle in the fridge."

"I'm good. I have a stakeout later on and don't want too much kidney activity to distract from nailing that sonofabitch from poking his wife's stepsister. He's so lazy he couldn't look beyond the family to scratch his tiny pecker's itch."

Sam flicked Lisa a smile. "The poetry of your words is pure pleasure to the listening ear."

"Thank you." Lisa's mouth lifted at one corner. "Anyway, I figured this Madison girl wants to hide from her mother, a nurse, and that set the hamster on the wheel running." Lisa raised a circling index finger to her head. "So I dig deeper. My digging turns up the fact Madison had a baby at seventeen. The baby died hours after birth but not before her mother had her sign the adoption papers against her will. Or so claims the nurse I spoke to."

"Christ, that would leave anyone emotionally scarred for life." Sam played with the lid of her water bottle.

"Do I sense sympathy radiating from The Piranha?"

Sam looked at Lisa. "What have I told you about calling me that?"

"To say it only in public. Isn't it enough I, Lisa McDonald, single-handedly branded you The Piranha, and you are now regarded as such in legal circles? Much better than The Rabid Badger moniker you came up with. I'm better than any marketing department. Mike drop." Lisa blew a pink bubble.

How Lisa was still single was a mystery, Sam thought when she deflated the gum bubble and sucked it back in with a slurping sound.

"That explains why Madison wants to distance herself from her mother and start a new life away from her. Anger and resentment are powerful emotions." Lisa slumped on the chair and slung an arm over its back.

"It is. Considering what she's been through, she seems rather grounded." Sam steepled fingers under her chin and fell deep in thought. "Do we know who got her pregnant?"

Lisa shook her head. "Do you want me to find out?"

"I do. It may be something or nothing, but she was only fifteen when she got pregnant. Maybe she needs closure, and I'd like to give her that."

"You've taken a shine to this girl."

Sam shook her head. "Lily has, and I need to know more about her. My gut tells me there's a lot more to her story."

Lisa's gum had reached maximum stretching capacity, and her bubble this time was twice as large. "I'll keep digging, boss. As far as the sequence of numbers you gave me. I've narrowed it down to a bank account. I'm going to need a bit more time."

"To track down the bank?"

"Naw. That's easy enough. There are only a few competing banks in Canada but many branches. I will need more time to find out which branch, and if that doesn't work, have my computer guru hack into the bank's system without leaving a trace." Lisa looked at Sam and saw something in her face that made her immediately jump in to correct what she'd said. "Backward record scratch on that. Wrong choice of words. Not hack. Nuh-uh, not hack. Never. I will need more time to find its owner or owners and the corresponding balances."

Sam gave Lisa an arched look. "All right, let me know when you get something." Sam glanced at her watch. "Madison's my next appointment and should be here soon. Good work, Lisa."

Lisa sucked in the bubble covering part of her face. "It's all I give, boss and why you pay me the big bucks."

Chapter 18

IN SAM'S BUILDING'S lobby, Madison checked the directory board next to the elevators for Hallstead Law. Sam's office occupied the entire twentieth floor of the building. Boarding the first elevator to arrive on the ground floor, Sam pressed the button for the twentieth floor.

The elevator ride was smooth and seamless, with seven others dressed fashionably and professionally. The look said, pretentious downtown, and their expensive aftershaves and sweet-smelling perfumes mixed and painted the air of the small space. The muzak in the elevator played a musical rendition of Wind Beneath My Wings.

Madison stepped out of the elevator on the twentieth floor onto a plush, gray carpet with black swirls behind the curved desk where two receptionists were busy answering ringing telephones. Over their shoulders, on the mirrored wall, the words Hallstead Law in bold, black letters greeted guests. The cacophony of office life echoed: staff chatted, people with files in their hands rushed to meetings, fingers tapped keyboards, and printers buzzed.

Madison checked in at the reception and was told by the older of the two receptionists to wait in the waiting area until called. Two other people were waiting to be called on the long burgundy leather sofa, and another visitor sat at one of the two matching chairs separated by a large square table. All wore polished suits, had impressive briefcases, and were on their cell phones conducting conversations that sounded pressing and vital to their existence.

Madison felt out of place in her leggings and tank top. Madison regretted not raiding Amber's closet after she left with Lily. Madison decided to stop at the mall on her way home to pick up a few items. It was time she stopped "borrowing" from Amber and had her own things. Madison had money to spend on luxuries like clothes to make herself presentable for such occasions, but she'd make Amber pay just the same. Madison wasn't there to take advantage of Amber, but she would get what she was owed.

Frowning, Madison pulled her ringing phone out of her purse, read the display, and swore. Everyone in the waiting area was too involved in their telephone conversation to react to her oath-laced rant.

"Hello, Mother."

"Where have you been, Madison? You haven't answered my calls or written me. I don't know whether you're dead or alive." Lacy's voice sounded neither fretful nor concerned.

"Like you care, Mother." Madison rose and walked away from the crowded waiting area.

"Of course, I care. You're my daughter. Where are you? How are you?"

Madison heard the crunching of the chip Lacy bit. "I'm fine, Mother. I have my own place and work at a great job."

"Good, good to hear. Where are you living? Where are you working?" Lacy bit into another chip.

"That's not important," Madison said, not that she'd tell her mother.

"How did you find out about the money in my account?" Lacy asked after a floating silence.

And there it was. The reason her mother was so concerned about her. Madison let out a quiet sigh. "You should rethink 1-2-3-4-5-6 as your password." In the background, Lacy heard the faint voice of a woman calling Madison's name. "I have to go. My lawyer is ready to meet with me."

"Christ, Madison. What are you doing meeting with a lawyer?" Lacy's voice rose in panic.

"What I should have done long ago." Madison hung up on her mother and muted the cell phone.

Chapter 19

THE TALL BRUNETTE walked up to Madison, introduced herself as Jenny and requested that she follow her. She wore a stylish black dress with a gold zipper that ran the length of her shapely back. Her expertly made-up hair and face made Madison feel inadequate and ordinary in her leggings and tank top. Madison pulled the hoodie tight around her to cover herself.

Jenny led Madison through the busy office buzzing with activity to a large corner office lit bright with sunlight pouring through the windows from all angles. The room smelled faintly of Chanel, and the woman sitting at the chair behind the desk was as impressive as the space she occupied.

Jenny offered Madison something to drink, which she turned down, and left the office, closing the door behind her back.

"Hello, Madison. Please have a seat." Sam gestured to the chocolate-brown sofa. "I'm surprised it's so busy here on a Saturday." Madison watched Sam round her desk and walk toward her. She wore a white sleeveless dress and floral Prada slingback pumps, and her red hair flowed in thick, shiny curls to her shoulders.

"Luckily for us, crime doesn't take a day off." Sam sat at the chair across her and crossed her long, toned legs. "Now, as I said on the telephone, I don't have much to report. It's only been a few days."

"Yes, you said, but any communication we have, no matter how trivial, I'd prefer to do it in person rather than over the telephone because you never know who's listening." Madison sat ramrod straight and rested folded hands on her lap. "And I appreciate you agreeing to use the burner cell phone to contact me."

"Not that I haven't done it before, but you do make things interesting. I'm just...."

Madison held up a hand before Madison finished her thought. "To put your mind at rest, I'd never hurt or put Lily in harm's way," Madison assured Sam.

"It never crossed my mind," Sam gave Madison a look out of solemn blue eyes.

"If this, between you and me, is going to work, I need you to be honest. I need to be able to trust you." Madison's tone was firm.

"All right. Professionally, you can trust me. You're my client, and I'm your lawyer, but I will admit I'm concerned about you being Lily's caretaker. Did Amber even vet you? Sometimes she could be...."

"Amber knows me well from years back. I needed a job and came to her asking for one. We're helping one another." Madison dropped her gaze, a telltale sign of lying by Sam's expert observation.

Sam rose and walked to the coffee machine on the sideboard. "If we're being honest, I don't believe a word you tell me. I've been friends with Amber forever, and Amber never mentioned you to me. Coffee? It won't be as good as yours, but it's drinkable."

"No, thanks. I don't have much time to spare. I need to get back home to make dinner for Lily and Amber. I'm not much of a cook, and making anything takes me a long time. And as far as Amber not mentioning me, everyone has secrets they hold close to them. I'm sure you do."

Sam looked at Madison and gave her a raised brow look. "I don't have untold personal secrets because I have nothing to hide." Sam inserted a vanilla latte pod into the coffee machine and pressed the button to set it to brew. Coffee spurted and filled the office with its scent. "By the way, where is Lily now?"

"She's with Amber. At the last minute, Amber volunteered to take Lily to the carnival at the mall to see the petting zoo I'd scheduled for this morning."

Brows furrowed in confusion. "Wait, Amber took the day off from work to take Lily to a mall carnival to pet animals."

Madison waved a hand in the air. "Thank you. So it's not just me that thought it out of the norm for Amber to volunteer."

Sam rolled her eyes. "Pfft, no, not normal. I can't remember when the last time was that Amber took a day off work."

"Well, this is the second day she's taken off in the past few weeks. She insisted on taking Lily for lunch and shopping to have a girl's day out with her. My guess is she'll be back home sooner than later. Amber's never spent so much time with Lily, and that little girl is full of energy."

Sam walked back to her chair with the cup of coffee in her hand. "She is that."

"It's why I'd like to get back soon."

"Yes, of course you do." Sam set aside speculating about Amber's bizarre behaviour rattling in her head and looked at Madison. "As I said, I have nothing to tell you except that my investigator believes the sequence of numbers you gave me is for a bank account. She's working on locating it and its owner." Sam slanted a look at a silent, unmoved Madison. "You know who it belongs to, don't you?"

Madison shook her head at Sam. "I don't. I suspect."

"Care to share what you know? The more you tell us, the quicker we'll get answers."

"Not yet. Not until you confirm the details." Madison rose and handed Sam a piece of paper inked with a brief notation.

Sam's blue eyes studied Madison carefully. "What's this?"

"I suspect that may help you locate the accounts."

Madison never failed to draw Sam's attention. "I'm your lawyer, Madison. You need to tell me what's going on here."

"I promise I will when the time is right."

Sam's intrigued eyes followed Madison out her office door.

Chapter 20

SHIT WAS GOING to hit the fan—soon. Sam would put it together as Madison hoped she would. The breadcrumbs Madison was dropping on Sam's lap like a chain reaction would lead to her story. Everything would come to light. Madison would tell Sam everything and let the chips fall where they may.

The truth would be out, and Madison would get what was rightfully hers. The dumpster fire that was Madison's life would be doused with facts. People would have to answer for what they did to her. Amber and her mother would pay. Everyone would. Madison would make sure of that.

Madison had been riding this crazy train for too long. Madison had gone through the spectrum of emotions for the past few years. The deception, anger, resentment, hate, despair, and confusion that balled into a massive solid ball in Madison's stomach and gripped her life had been there for too long.

And today was no exception, but Madison had things to do. She needed to shop for a new outfit to look her best for Hunter tonight.

Madison never considered herself a shopper or fashion-wise and detested clothes shopping. A blessing when you're broke, but thanks to Amber, she wasn't anymore. Madison took a right at the next intersection.

Shopping at the exclusive boutiques on Bloor Street is what Madison would do before heading home.

MADISON WORE HOME THE SHORT BLACK dress with the knee-high boots with spiked heels she bought. Slung on her shoulder was the tote that matched the boots she picked up at the Michael Kors store.

Madison had her hair cut and styled at the salon across from the Michael Kors store. Before leaving the salon, Madison took advantage of the makeup artist's offer. Her eyes were shadowed metallic-gray and lined Cleopatra style. Her cheeks were dusted blush pink, and her lips were glossy crimson. Madison felt feminine, beautiful, and happy. Madison bought every product used.

Whoever said money didn't buy happiness was a moron?

When Madison walked into the kitchen, Amber swivelled her head and cast eyes on the woman looking cover girl worthy. Knocked back by Madison's striking appearance, there was a long pause as speechless Amber, wide-eyed and open-mouthed, stared at Madison.

"Wow, Madison. You look beautiful." Lily's voice lingered on the beautiful as Bessie barked in agreement.

"You think so?" Madison pushed her hair back over her shoulder.

"Yeah. Doesn't she look beautiful, Mommy?"

Amber silently nodded as her mind raced. Where had Madison been all morning? Who was the friend she said she was meeting, and for what reason?

Hunter was the friend Madison met, and Amber knew precisely for what reason. She felt it in her gut. That's what Hunter and Madison talked about last night by the pool, or mainly Madison did because Amber was sure she was the seducer.

Madison was with Hunter all morning, screwing his brains out. Amber's paranoia was feeding on itself.

"Yes, she looks great. Your meeting must have been with someone special," Amber said with probing eyes.

"Not really." Madison laid a hand on the counter's edge and raised her foot to remove her boot. She repeated the motion with the opposite hand and pulled the other boot off. "I'm not used to high heels, and these boots are killing my feet. You're home early. I wasn't expecting you back until late afternoon."

Amber watched Madison casually stroll to the sink to fill a glass with water. How could she be so casual in her home, around her and her daughter, after spending the morning with Hunter?

"I got sick," Lily proudly announced, her short legs swinging back and forth on the chair.

"Yes, Lily got sick," Amber said, watching Madison reach into her new handbag for her phone that hadn't stopped buzzing since she walked in. "Someone seems anxious to get a hold of you."

Madison read the screen. Fifteen missed calls from her mother. "It's no one important." She tossed the phone back into the handbag and turned to Lily. "Let me guess. This little sugar monster talked you into buying her too much sugary stuff. She flashed you a pouty, imploring look that broke you. Didn't you, you little trickster?" Madison touched the tip of Lily's nose with her finger. "And Mommy gave in to you, and you got sick."

Because Amber now felt stupid for being taken by her five-year-old daughter, she remained silent.

Lily's look was one of pure mischief. "I throwed up next to Mommy's car, right on the wheel. It was yucky. Then Bessie started licking it."

Madison stifled the smile. "It's threw up, and I imagine it was very yucky, and you, Bessie, are a yucky dog."

Bessie plopped her butt on the floor and looked up with a doggie grin.

"Mommy took the car to wash it because it stunk, and she didn't want you to know it stunk."

"Okay, that's enough talk of being sick." Amber cut Lily off.

"You won't do it again. Will you?" Madison asked.

Lily shook her head. "No, I won't. I didn't like the throw-up."

Madison winked at Lily. "Good call, peanut. Now, play with Bessie in your room while I get the chicken soup on."

"I don't want chicken soup." Lily looked down at Bessie as if conferring with the dog. "Bessie doesn't either."

"You will later, and your upset tummy will thank you. Now, go on."

"Okay, Madison. Let's go, Bessie. We're going to have a tea party."

"You do look great, Madison. Hard to believe you got this dolled up for 'just a friend.'" Amber pursued the conversation again in the hope of getting answers.

"I didn't." Madison reached into the refrigerator for the chicken and the vegetables she needed to make the soup. "I went shopping after my meeting, which by the way, you're paying for."

"Of course I am. I'm not a money pit, you know." Ice dripped from Amber's words.

"I'm not greedy, Amber. I couldn't bring myself to buy everything I wanted, which I should have because you owe me. Being the decent human being I am, I only bought this outfit. That guilt thing gets in the way for me in the way it doesn't for you, or you wouldn't have done what you did." Madison aimed blue eyes at Amber once she set the pot of water on the stove.

Amber dismissed the jab. "Were you at the restaurant this morning?"

Madison added chicken to the pot. "What are you talking about?"

"Answer the question." Defiance ripe in Amber's eyes, she snapped, "Were you at Hunter's restaurant this morning?"

"No. Why would I be?" Madison added two peeled cloves of garlic, celery stalks, and peeled carrots to the pot. "I like it better when you go to work. It's quieter around here when you do." Madison mumbled, adding salt and pepper to the soup mixture.

"You're lying."

"I'm not. I need to change into more comfortable clothes. Don't worry about the pot on the stove. I'll be right back. Don't let Lily into the kitchen unsupervised."

"What were you and Hunter talking about last night? I saw the two of you talking by the pool." Amber caught Madison's attention, and she paused at the door. "I watched you from our bedroom window."

Madison heard the jealousy pulsing in Amber's voice. "We were talking about nothing of consequence."

"Turn around. Look at me when you say that."

Madison turned and looked Amber straight in the eyes. Thoughts she couldn't stop, things she wanted to say, rolled through Madison's mind in an endless loop. Madison debated. Should she tell Amber the truth about Hunter? Amber had a right to know—everything.

Madison opted to say nothing. She could get money out of Hunter as well as Amber.

"He asked me if I enjoyed dinner and how the service was."

"Why would he care what you think?"

"I was a server at the restaurant, or have you forgotten? Talk, that's all it was, Amber." Madison kept her eyes on Amber. "Believe me when I tell you, I have zero interest in Hunter."

Jealousy clouded rationality, and Amber gave in to her black temper. "You want me to believe that? You want me to believe he's not part of your plan to take everything you can from me. I see the way you look at him. He's handsome, successful, and wealthy." Nerves grinding, Amber fished for the pack of cigarettes from the utility drawer. Amber set the package down when Madison frowned.

"Get this through your head, Amber. Hunter is all those things in your eyes, not mine. I have no interest in Hunter."

Amber didn't get a ring of sincerity in Madison's voice. "That's not what I saw last night."

She laughed bitterly. "This may come as a news flash, Amber, but only you see Hunter through perfect lenses. Love, fear, lack of confidence, something has you so blinded you don't see the man I see."

"What's that supposed to mean?"

"Just that, Amber. He's not the perfect man, you see. His money is yours, and his successes are yours, not his. From what I heard this morning, you're the one financing Hunter," Madison told Amber to drive the point home.

Temper whipped colour into Amber's face. "You were listening in on our private conversation?"

"They're hardly a private conversation when they're loud enough to project through your bedroom door."

Amber gaped at Madison. "You have no right to listen in on my conversation with my husband."

"I couldn't care less what you and Hunter talk about. If truth were told, Amber, I'd rather not hear you. Your conversations leave me feeling sorry for you."

"What the hell is that supposed to mean?"

Madison took a step, stopped, and turned to Amber. "Open your eyes, Amber. Only then will you see the truth," she said, leaving the kitchen.

Chapter 21

AT TEN O'CLOCK, Amber's bedroom darkened, and Madison snuck out of her house. She crept through the trees and around the side of the house to the front. Three doors down, in front of Esposito's house, Madison got into the Uber car she ordered. Madison couldn't risk Amber hearing the loud muffler of her car back out of the driveway and finding out she was stepping out for the night.

Few cars were heading north on the highway. However, southbound traffic en route to the downtown core was bumper to bumper as the Saturday night revellers looked for entertainment. Considering the traffic congestion, Madison gave herself extra travelling time. Madison looked forward to tonight and didn't want to risk being late.

The Uber driver, a thirtysomething Formula One wannabe, got Madison to Hunter's waterfront apartment in record time, and Madison arrived one hour before her midnight rendezvous time with Hunter.

On the penthouse floor of the building, Madison found the key Hudson left under the hallway console table and let herself into the apartment. Madison flipped the light switch, and the ceiling lights shone brightly. Madison surveyed the apartment.

It was a spacious loft-style space. The floor was Italian marble, white and gleaming. The walls were

brownish-gray with stunning artwork. Originals were Hunter's style. The sofas and chairs were Italian leather, and the tables were dark oak. A thick tan pile carpet covered the living room area, and a large flat screen hung on a wall above black floating shelves. Black lacquer wall cabinets, counters, and stainless steel appliances were the décor of choice in the kitchen. Counters were white, and a wine rack was stocked with hundreds of bottles from around the world.

Walking to the refrigerator, Madison opened the door and reached for the bottle of champagne she knew would be there for her—a predictable Hunter move. Madison popped the cork and poured it into the crystal glass she retrieved from the cupboard.

Madison sipped champagne and clucked her tongue. "Yummy." She wasn't a champagne connoisseur by any stretch of the imagination, but knowing Hunter, that was an expensive mouthful.

Madison reached into her MK handbag for her buzzing phone and saw more calls and text messages from her mother. She ignored all.

Madison texted: I'm at the apartment, drinking excellent champagne and waiting for you. Don't keep me waiting long.

Madison's cell phone rang seconds after she sent the text.

"I've been calling you," Hunter said with unusual sharpness.

"I'm sorry. I had my phone muted." The calls from her mother had become incessant, and Madison wanted none of it. "When are you getting here? I've already started drinking and can't wait to get this party started."

Hunter heaved a sigh that sounded like regret. "That's why I've been calling. I can't make it tonight. Lily's sick and has been asking for me. I have to get home. If I don't, Amber will nag and nag. Nagging is what she lives for."

From the glass wall, Madison could see the waterfront. Party boats lit up with string lights cruised in black water under a moon sliced in half, its glow sharp in the dark sky showered with stars.

"She has a tummy ache. Amber gave her too much candy to eat at the carnival." Madison made sure to point the blame at Amber.

"Goddamn, Amber," Hunter said so sharply it put a gratified smile on Madison's face.

"It's a tummy ache. Lily will survive."

The air hummed between them for a moment as Hunter debated getting in his car and making the drive to the apartment. Duty prevailed. "No, I can't make it. I have to go home."

"But…."

"You enjoy yourself. Go down to the pool. Take a sauna and a whirlpool." Hunter fished his car keys from his pants pocket.

"I wasn't planning on wearing anything. I didn't bring my bathing suit."

She drove a spike of lust into his gut. "Christ, I just got hard for you."

"Mmm, you know I can do so many things with that." Madison slurped her drink.

Hunter's pulsed hammered when his imagination ran wild. He debated some more. There was a momentary lapse of control before sound reasoning took over, and he mustered all his strength to say, "No. No, I can't. Amber will be on my back like a bad rash if I don't go home.

You'll find a selection of bathing suits and towels in the hallway closet."

"Fine, I'll have to take care of myself. Think of that while you're driving home." Her breathy voice drove the image into his mind, and heat centred in a ball in his gut.

"Jesus, baby, you made me harder, and now I'm going to have to take care of myself."

"I want to do that," Madison murmured.

"Jesus! You got me so horny right now." Hunter's breath was unsteady. "But, no, I need to go home."

"Okay, fine." Madison's voice was laced with disappointment.

"Don't worry, baby. We'll get together soon. Very soon."

"I'll wait for your call." Madison hung up and went in search of a bathing suit.

Changing into the polka dot bikini Madison chose from the collection Hunter kept in the closet, she threw on a zebra print cover-up and reached for a towel. Madison let out a long sigh and set off to do what she'd come to Hunter's apartment to do.

Madison spotted the hidden camera when entering the apartment and didn't put it past Hunter to have them throughout. Assuming he was watching her every move, Madison put on a show in the skimpy bikini for him. Mission accomplished, Madison shut the lights off to make the apartment dark and avoid further camera detection. Next, Madison set the alarm.

The only sound in the apartment was the beeping alarm as it activated.

Opening the entry door to the apartment, Madison held it for a moment to simulate her departure on the alarm system before she closed it from the inside.

Madison hoped loosening the light bulbs on the hallway lights prevented the cameras from picking up anything but blackness.

Madison put on the night vision goggles she ordered online in the darkened apartment and headed down the hallway toward Hunter's office. She planned to search it first, the living room next, and the bedroom last. After seeing the wide-open lay of the living room and how sparsely furnished it was, she nixed the idea and determined there were few places to hide anything.

The bedroom at the top of the winding staircase overlooking the living room would come next.

Slipping her gloves on, Madison turned the office door handle. Locked. Luckily, she planned for such an inconvenience and brought the necessary tools. Madison hoped the YouTube videos on how to pick a lock were accurate.

As Madison inserted the pick at the top of the lock, she thought it amazing how easily tonight came together. There might be a place for her in espionage.

Seducing Hunter was easier than Madison anticipated. Toss sex into the equation, and men become weak fools. Sex was every man's kryptonite, and Hunter would never suspect she was playing him. The man was as stupid as he was good-looking, and Madison would nail his ass to the wall and own him and everything he owned.

Madison set the tension wrench into the bottom of the keyhole and jiggled it. It didn't work. Calmly Madison reversed the process. Tension wrench into the bottom of the keyhole first, then pick at the top of the lock. Et voila!

Throwing the office door open, Madison studied the room carefully. Straight ahead was a glass-top desk with a laptop, a landline telephone, and two Montblanc on a pen holder. A black, leather executive chair was pushed against the desk.

A credenza to its right had a silver tray with a decanter of whiskey, two glasses, and a silver ice bucket. A Tiffany lamp stood next to the tray. A black leather briefcase on the leather sofa with the words HUNTER ROCHE embossed in gold caught Madison's attention. She walked to it and opened it. It was empty, just like Hunter to have something merely for show.

Madison fired up the laptop. As she suspected, it opened to an empty screen. Hunter wouldn't know how to turn it on or use it. It was there as intellectual ornamentation.

Madison walked to the credenza and found the drawers locked. That had her winging her brow. Secrets were kept behind lock and key, and she picked the lock. Thank you, YouTube, Madison thought when she successfully picked the lock.

Madison opened the drawer and flipped through the hanging folders. She wasn't wrong about discovering secrets and reached for the cell phone concealed in the towel to take photographs of the documents she found. Madison took some original invoices and statements for proof, enough not to raise Hunter's attention.

Done searching the office, Madison took one last look to ensure she left everything as she found it. Satisfied she had, Madison headed up the winding staircase to the bedroom.

Walking to the dresser, Madison went through the dresser drawers. Socks neatly folded were set in six colour-coded rows. The underwear drawer was as primly arranged as the socks. So was the undershirt drawer. That

Hunter was fastidious, and obsessive was an understatement.

Going through all the drawers, Madison came up empty.

Next, Madison checked under the bed covered in red Egyptian cotton and a stack of pillows. There wasn't a dust mote in sight or anything of interest.

Madison crossed to the closet and slid the doors open. Shirts, pants, T-shirts, and jeans, all designer and expensive, were hung on wooden hangers half an inch apart.

In the closet, Madison found nothing of interest. That is until she found the stepladder hidden behind a tall box, and her alarm bell went off because who kept a stepladder in the closet?

Madison stepped back and, for a long while, studied the closet.

The silence was smothering.

Then it hit her.

Climbing the stepladder, Madison knocked on the wall above the shelf. It was hollow. Madison pulled out her cell phone and took pictures of the stacked shelf for later reference.

Moving the boxes aside, Madison saw the handle painted the same colour as the steel-blue wall and smoothly flush. Unless you were looking for it, you'd fail to see it.

Reaching for the handle, Madison pulled it. The right side panel came loose, and she saw the boxes.

Madison's lips curved into a smile. She found what she was looking for. Staring at her find, Madison fell into reverent silence.

With quick precision, Madison dug out the one thing she was interested in. Referencing the earlier photograph on her phone, Madison returned everything to its rightful place. Hunter would never know she was there.

Back downstairs, by the entry door, Madison checked her watch. It was forty-five minutes since she'd supposedly gone for her swim and whirlpool. Wrapping the night goggles in the towel, Madison opened the door. She turned the alarm off and flicked the lights on.

In the living room, wrapped in a guest robe, her hair in long, wet ropes, Madison poured herself a glass of champagne. She dimmed the lights. A haze of moonlight floated through the glass wall into the apartment. Madison turned the stereo on. Hunter was an old-fashioned guy. Vinyl under a needle was his style.

It took Madison a few tries to figure out how to work the stereo. When she did, the soulful, soothing sound of The Commodores flowed from the speakers. Hunter was a romantic. Too bad he was such a dick.

Stretching out on the sofa, with Lionel Ritchie singing passionately about playing the games that people play, Madison sipped on champagne and enjoyed the view of the city studded like one giant searchlight lighting up the night sky.

She could get used to this. Yes, siree, Bob, this was the life Madison was meant to live, and it soon would all be hers. Revenge was a powerful motivator, and Karma was a bitch named Madison Donnell.

Chapter 22

SATISFIED WITH THE outcome of last night's fact-finding mission, Madison made her way up the stairs to Lily's room with a smile. Madison would hold on to the information she uncovered at Hunter's apartment and turn it over to Sam when the time was right. Madison would own Hunter and Amber's ass as it should be, as she had plotted to do for the past year.

We are our actions, and Hunter and Amber should hurt as much as Madison did.

Madison wouldn't have to put much effort into crushing Hunter. Sam would do it for her. Sam detested the man, and when Madison showed her what she found at the apartment, it would set her off like a rabid dog after Hunter.

As for Amber, Madison aimed to take everything dear to her. She would kill her relationship with Sam, her only friend. Sam would react with shock, betrayal, and horror when Madison exposed who the woman she trusted and loved was. Madison would take everything she deserved from Amber: her home, money, and daughter.

Madison loved Lily more than life itself, and she had become attached to the grand living and the lifestyle that came with it. Everything Amber had would be Madison's by the time she was finished.

Madison wished she could see Lacy's face when she found out, but she wouldn't. Lacy wouldn't set foot in her home or her new life. As far as Madison was concerned, Lacy was as complicit as Amber and Hunter and was dead to Madison.

Walking toward Lily's bedroom to get her out of bed and dressed, Madison stopped at Amber's bedroom when she heard Hunter's raised voice. She pressed her ear to the door.

"Christ, Amber, do you always have to be so fucking melodramatic about everything?" Hunter's clipped voice put a smile on Madison's face.

Amber deserved every bit of Hunter's anger.

"For the third time, Hunter, I didn't text you last night. I don't even know where my cell phone is," said Amber flipping the bedsheets for her phone.

Madison heard drawers opening and slamming shut and thought what a ditz Amber was.

"Goddamn it, Amber, I left the restaurant to rush home on a Saturday night. Do you know how busy I was?" Irritation edged into Hunter's voice.

If only Amber knew the truth, she was as deceitful as Hunter.

"Keep your voice down, and please stop swearing. Lily will hear you." Amber rummaged through the contents on the dresser. "Where is that phone?"

"I dropped everything and rushed home for my daughter's tummy ache because you made it sound like she was dying."

"Once again, I didn't text you."

Hunter held his cell phone to Amber's face to show her the text. "What's this?"

Amber read the message. Lily's really, really sick. She's asking for her daddy. Come home as soon as you can. We both need you. A heart emoji followed.

"It seems to be a text from me, but I didn't send it, Hunter. Someone is playing with you. Where's that goddamn phone so I can prove to you I didn't send you anything." Amber tossed the bedsheets back. Nothing.

"Christ, Amber, is that the best you can do? The text fairies sent it." Hunter's harsh tone made Madison's grin widen. There was nothing more satisfying than instigating a rift between Amber and Hunter.

"Please, Hunter, keep your voice down. I don't want Lily to hear us arguing."

The sexual frustration from his conversation with Madison still gnawing at Hunter, he gave in to temper. "I don't give a shit, Amber. The girl needs to know how useless a mother she has. And useless you are, Amber, you always have been." Hunter's temper flared.

"I'm sorry, Hunter. I didn't mean to upset you," Amber said, low-voiced, her tone sounding defeated.

"And yet you have—again. I can't stand the sight of you." There was disdain in his voice.

"Please, Hunter, don't be upset with me." The tears came in sobs.

"Save the tears, Amber. Do you know how repulsive you are?" Madison's beaming smile flattened when she heard the backhanded slap and Amber's whimper. "I'm going to work."

"But it's Sunday, and the restaurant's closed today." Amber sounded pitiful.

Madison could hear the abject fear, helplessness, and fragility in Amber's voice. Madison's thin shoulders hunched. No one knows what others are going through or how they got there. Madison thought.

"I need to be far away from you, and don't expect me home tonight." Hunter's snide words were the last

Madison heard before she broke away from the door and sprinted to Lily's room.

Part III

The End

Sometimes the world has light, hope, and love.

—M.L. Lexi

Chapter 23

THE SCENT OF brewing coffee, baking cookies, and blueberry pancakes came to Amber when she walked into the kitchen. Madison flipped the pancakes on the grill while Lily, with Bessie, kept an eye on the baking cookies in the oven through the glass window.

"Good morning, Mommy," Lily said cheerily. She wore an orange T-shirt, purple leggings, lemon-yellow ankle socks, and blue sandals—all of Lily's choosing. Expressing her individualism, Madison said, was good for her artistic soul. "Madison and I made cookies, and I'm watching them grow until they get...."

"Golden brown," Madison finished when Lily looked at her.

"Yeah. They should be ready soon, and then we'll have them with milk." Bessie added a keen bark. "You too, Bessie," Lily assured and put an arm over Bessie's shoulders as both watched the cookies brown in the oven.

"They smell wonderful, baby." Amber forced a smile as she poured herself a cup of coffee. "I can't wait to taste them."

"Us too," Lily said without taking her eyes off the oven window.

"Aren't you going to work today, Amber?" Madison eyed the gray sweatpants, baggy sweatshirt, and the hair loosely clinched with a purple clip.

"Maybe, later." The sullen expression on Amber's face spoke volumes.

"This is the third time you've left late for work this week."

"What's it to you?"

Amber's reply caused Madison to lift a brow. "Maybe the blueberry pancakes I made for you will put you in a better mood. Have a seat, Amber. They'll be ready in a few minutes." Madison walked butter and maple syrup to the table and set them before Amber.

Amber stared at Madison. "You made blueberry pancakes?"

Madison pressed the top of the pancakes with her finger to check the bounce. "Uh-huh."

"They're my favourite."

"I know. You've said so on your show." Madison glanced at Amber. She had done a good job covering the bruise where Hunter slapped her face with makeup, but Madison could see she'd been crying under the thick, black eyeliner.

A pang of guilt hit Madison.

Madison blamed herself for what happened to Amber. Her deceit caused Hunter to raise his hand to Amber.

Madison's hands went into tight fists.

Hunter had no right to lay a hand on Amber, but Madison was why he had.

Madison's fists tightened and her nails dug welts on her skin. She sucked in her breath and exhaled it. "Can I get you more coffee?"

Amber's brows pressed together in what looked like puzzlement. "Thank you."

Madison plated two pancakes, picked up the coffee pot and brought both to the table. "I know it's a lot of carbs, but once in a while, you must treat yourself. You should add the butter now while the pancakes are hot." Madison walked back to the sink, reached in for the dishes soaking in soapy water and rinsed.

Outside, flashes of lightning that lit up the gray sky followed the rumble of thunder. Dark clouds heavy with water opened, and the rain came down hard. Rain pattered on the window in a continuous motion. Madison watched the raindrops cling to the windowpane in beads and fuse with others as they slid down and disappeared when they hit the brick ledge.

From the reflection on the window, Madison caught Amber rubbing her temple, hoping to relieve the pressure from the pounding headache triggered by Hunter's slap.

Setting the last washed dish on the rack, Madison reached into the drawer for the bottle of Tylenol and popped two into her hand. "Take both."

Amber's eyebrows lift in wonder. "Why are you being so nice to me? Today blueberry pancakes, yesterday you made waffles, and the day before, you made me a banana-strawberry smoothie, all favourites of mine."

"I'm a nice person." Madison screwed the lid back on the Tylenol bottle. "Go ahead, take them."

Amber popped the Tylenol pills into her mouth and chased them with coffee. "I ask again, why are you being so nice?"

It took her a moment for Amber to put it together. The idea that Madison knew what Hunter did, had embarrassment and shame burning to the sickness in Amber's stomach. Madison would add the knowledge to her arsenal to use against her. She would make it public, and the world would know the disorder that was her life.

Her competition would jockey up to take her show from her, and she would lose everything she'd worked hard for.

Madison saw the flicker of knowing in Amber's eyes and watched the slow flush work its way up her throat to her cheeks. When the shame waned, anger slid in, and Amber looked at Madison with eyes hard as stone.

Madison held her hand up, palm out to silence Amber when she opened her mouth to speak. "The cookies are done, peanut."

"But the stove hasn't dinged," Lily said, and Bessie barked.

"It will, in a couple of seconds." Madison turned the timer off and slid her hand into an oven mitt. "See, they're golden brown," she said, pulling the tray out of the oven. "As soon as they're cool enough to eat, I'll bring you and Bessie a cookie. For now, take your glass of milk, and you and Bessie go watch television in the office."

"But Mommy and Daddy said I'm not allowed in the office." Lily reached for the cup of milk Madison held out to her.

"You're allowed just for today. Now go on. Turn the television on to channel two. Dora The Explorer should be on now." Madison patted Lily on her behind to send her on her way.

"Okay. Come on, Bessie."

When Lily left the kitchen, Madison said, "Has Hunter done that before?"

"You force your way into my home. You're here not by my choice, not for want, and now you meddle in my and my husband's affairs. You have no right to interfere." Amber's voice pitching high, she barked with indignation.

Madison heard a lot in Amber's voice and saw the tangles of anger, resentment, embarrassment, and shame that crossed Amber's face.

Madison scraped back the chair beside Amber and sat. "Has Hunter done this before?"

Amber shut her eyes and bowed her head.

Madison's hand closed over Amber's. "This isn't the first time he's laid a hand on you, is it?"

"You have no right to listen in on our private conversations." Amber's voice was barely a whisper.

"Look at me, Amber. Tell me the truth."

Amber took a steadying breath, and her head rose to meet Madison's eyes. For a long silent moment, their eyes held on one another. No words had to be said for Madison to recognize the humiliation and shame in Amber for something, not of her making and not deserved.

The confident, successful woman Madison had watched on television for months while nursing her hatred and plotting her revenge to strip her of everything she was, everything she owned, looked small and vulnerable, broken.

Madison wasn't expecting this. Her first instinct was to feel sorry for Amber. Not the reaction Madison expected to have after what Amber did to her. But here she was.

Madison's face softened. "This is not your fault, Amber. Hunter has no right to lay a hand on you, no matter what."

Amber stared at her folded hands as if a message might be communicated to her through them.

"You don't need to put up with this shit from him, Amber." Madison gave in to her anger.

"Madison, are the cookies cold enough to eat? Bessie and I are hungry." Lily called from the office.

"They are, peanut. I'll be right there." Madison turned to Amber. "Stay put. We're not done talking."

"Sit down, Amber," Madison said when she returned to the kitchen and found Amber by the terrace door.

Rain pattered in rhythmic, soothing drumming sound on the ground. Amber had always loved the smell of wet grass and how the rainfall ruffled the leaves on the trees and dimpled the surface of the lake water. Afterward, Amber liked how everything gleamed with rain and lent a romantic feel.

"Isn't it a little too early for that?" Amber said when she whirled to see Madison pouring Irish Cream into her coffee cup.

"Liquid courage has no timetable. Drink."

Amber picked up the cup and took a generous sip. The Irish Cream in her coffee was strong, with the amount of kick Amber needed. "He doesn't do it often."

Madison's head snapped up. "Once is too often."

The tears wanted to come, but Amber blinked them back. "He's my husband."

Madison widened her eyes and raised her eyebrows. "So fucking what? It doesn't give him the right to lay a hand on you, Amber."

Amber took a sizable, numbing gulp of her coffee. "There's no need to swear. Lily will hear you."

Madison topped up Amber's cup with coffee and more Irish Cream and poured one for herself. "How many times has the fucker done this?"

Amber said nothing.

"How do you keep it hidden from everyone? Christ, you're in front of a camera most days."

Amber took another hefty drink from her cup.

"Why do you put up with it? You're successful, educated, and way more accomplished than he'll ever be. This home, everything you have is your doing, not his. Why would you put up with his shit?"

"I love him." Amber kept her voice low.

Madison circled a finger in front of Amber's bruised face. "This is not love." Agitated, Madison stalked the room.

"Why do you care so much? If anything, this plays right into your plan, doesn't it?" Amber asked, keeping direct eyes on Madison.

Madison looked into Amber's swollen eyes. She was the cause of her tears, and the bruise beneath the thick layer of makeup and guilt gnawed at her with sharp blade-like teeth. "I only came here to get what's mine, what's owed to me. I never intended for anyone to get hurt."

"What are you talking about?" Amber stared dully.

Rain pounded on the ground, window, and the kitchen's glass doors. Streaks of lightning flashed across the sky, and the thunder followed.

Madison's face was solemn as she looked at Amber and said, "I sent Hunter the text about Lily being sick." The tears, the first in a long while, formed in Madison's eyes. "I'm sorry, Amber. Hunter did this to you because of me." The tears now streamed from Madison's eyes.

Chapter 24

DETERMINED TO REGAIN her calm and dignity, Madison wiped the tears from her face with her hands and drew a breath, a second, and a third.

"Why? Why would you send a text from my cell phone to Hunter?" Amber's jaw set tightly.

Madison gave Amber a look from under her lashes. "I can't tell you right now, but there's a reason and purpose."

"You can't tell me?" Amber's anger took over. "You send my husband a fictional text from my cell phone that results in this," she raised a finger to her face, "and you can't tell me."

Unable to look her in the eyes, Madison gave Amber her back and busied herself, making a fresh pot of coffee. "I never imagined he would do something like that."

"Well, he did." Amber's face filled with pure defiance. "Do I need to brace myself for more outbursts from Hunter instigated by you?"

Madison swirled to face Amber. "Of course not. What do you think I am?"

"I don't know who you are. Not really. I don't know what you want. Not exactly. You've been here a few weeks and haven't been honest with me."

Madison filled the coffee machine's reservoir with water, pressed the ON button, and soon watched the coffee spurt into the glass carafe.

"I will tell you everything soon." Madison turned to face Amber. "I'm not ready yet. There are a few things I need to piece together first."

"What does that mean?"

"Just that. I have nothing to say … yet."

"Christ, Madison, you sent Hunter a phoney text from my cell phone, which by the way, I'd like to know how you managed to unlock and tell me you can't tell me anything."

"You old people should consider another password other than 1-2-3-4-5-6."

"I'm thirty-three." Amber shot back sourly.

Madison brought the freshly brewed coffee to the table and refilled both cups. "Has he ever laid a hand on Lily?" Asking the questions had Madison's stomach flipping.

Amber closed her eyes. "No. I'd never allow it."

Madison's brows pressed together in what looked like doubt. "I hope not."

"I wouldn't."

Madison studied Amber for a moment. "Sorry, it's hard to believe when you allow him to do it to you. Why put up with verbal and physical abuse? Why not leave him? Hunter's no prize, Amber, and you don't need him."

"That's what I've been saying for the past ten years," Sam said from the doorway.

Both women turned to face her. She looked elegant in a white pantsuit against an orange blouse low enough to expose the swell of her breasts. Her red hair was a cloud of flowing curls around her striking face. She wore gold bangles at her wrist that jingled and a thick Cartier chain at her neck.

"How long have you been standing there, eavesdropping?" Amber asked.

"I don't eavesdrop. I listen, and long enough to have my suspicions confirmed." Sam sauntered over to the table and brought the sweet scent of her expensive perfume. "I've always suspected that sonofabitch was emasculated by you and was verbally and physically abusive, but I never had proof. She'd never admit it to me, her best friend, who has only her best interest at heart." Amber slid into a chair, picked up Amber's cup of coffee, and drank. "Christ! That's one part coffee, three parts Irish Cream."

"I'll get you a cup of straight coffee," Madison said.

"Don't you dare. This is perfect." Sam sipped some more.

"What's a son...? I can't remember the rest," Lily said, walking into the kitchen with Bessie at her heels.

The three women turned to Lily, but Sam answered her. "That word is an Auntie Sam word, and what have I said about Auntie Sam's words?"

"I can't repeat them," Lily said.

"That's right, baby." Sam touched her finger to the tip of Lily's nose. "You are not just a pretty face."

"Bessie wants to know if she's pretty too," Lily explained when Bessie rose on her hind legs and planted her paws on Sam's thighs.

"Of course, you're pretty too." Sam thrilled Bessie with head scratches, and her tail swished like helicopter propellers in excitement.

Lily let out a girlish giggle. "Did you bring me a present, Auntie Sam?"

"Not today, baby. The present I brought today is for your mother."

"Oh, okay." Lily's disappointment lasted for ten seconds. "Bessie and I are hungry again. We can eat another cookie."

"You speak for the both of you, do you?" Madison said, and Lily nodded.

"Bessie and me want chocolate milk with the cookies."

"You can have another cookie and a banana. Deal?" Amber said.

Lily considered. "Okay, deal, Mommy."

"Sesame Street should be coming on soon. Go watch it while Auntie Sam, Mommy, and I talk." Madison handed Lily the cookies and the smallest banana from the fruit basket.

"I'm allowed in Mommy and Daddy's office today." Lily flashed Sam a bright smile as she walked past.

Sam looked over at Amber. "Hopefully, your mommy will come to her senses and make it her office only."

Lily frowned slightly. "Huh?"

"Go on, peanut. I'll be in later to play with you." Madison walked Lily to the kitchen door.

"Okay, but can we have a tea party with Mommy, Auntie Sam, you, and Bessie?"

"We wouldn't miss it. Now, go on. Big Bird is waiting." Madison kissed Lily's head and watched the girl and dog leave the kitchen.

"I love that girl like my own, but I have to say her sense of fashion is sending out an S.O.S. beacon," Sam mumbled when Lily was out of earshot.

"Why do you say shit like that in front of Lily?" Amber huffed.

"Well, did you see the way she's dressed?"

"Not that, you judgmental prima donna. I'm talking about the, 'hopefully, your mommy will come to her senses and make it her office only' comment." Amber mimicked Sam's voice.

"There's no need for anger, and I say that because it's my wish, and it has been for years. Because I want you to see the woman you are, the woman you can be without that mooch, who also happens to be an abusive ass-wipe." Sam reached for the bottle of Irish Cream and poured it into the white mug Madison set before her.

"That's my husband you're talking about," Amber replied coolly.

"You may say differently after you see what I've uncovered about this wonderful husband of yours." Sam dropped the file she pulled out from her handbag on the table.

Chapter 25

AMBER FLICKED EYES from the manila folder on the table to Sam. "What's this?"

Sam sat back and crossed her arms. "It's information I've uncovered on Hunter during an

investigation I've conducted for a client."

Lily's laughter and Bessie's bark from the office filled the uncomfortable silence.

"Well, aren't you in the least bit curious?" Sam said, with Madison silently looking on.

"No." Amber pushed the folder away. "Who's the client?"

Sam looked at Amber with deadpan eyes. "You know I can't tell you that."

"No, you can't because it's you. You're the one running a background check on Hunter. Really, Sam, I didn't think you'd stoop so low. Are you so jealous of my and Hunter's relationship that you must destroy us?"

Sam remained stoic. A reaction or comment would incite resistance from Amber, and she wouldn't look at the file that contained information she needed to know, things she couldn't imagine existed.

"You're not in the least bit curious to see what's in that thick file?" Sam remained aloof.

Amber's head snapped up and flashed eyes full of anger at Sam. "Yes, I'm sure. I've told you repeatedly, for better or worse, he's my husband. You must stop going after Hunter and trying to turn me against him." Amber stared at Sam as her brows winged up. "You're so jealous I have the loving man you haven't found in my life. You resent me for having the steady, solid relationship you can only dream of."

Sam bit back the pfft at the tip of her tongue to not antagonize Amber further. "That couldn't be the farthest thing from the truth, and you know it."

Amber waved a silencing finger at Sam. "I'm not done. All you have are failed relationships with men who can't stand to be around you for longer than a one-night stand." Amber stood and walked to the patio doors to distance herself and Sam.

Madison started to speak but stopped when Sam signalled her not to speak.

"It's anger for Hunter, not for me, talking," Sam murmured to Madison.

"I want you to leave my house, Sam, and I don't want you coming back—ever. I mean it, Sam. I want you out of my house, my life, and Lily's life." Amber's eyes narrowed into slits.

Sam wasn't expecting that, and the shock stole her breath. "You can't be serious," Sam said when she got her breath back.

"I've never been more serious. Get out, Sam." Amber's arms wrapped around her as she looked out to the lake as she spoke.

The rain had stopped, but the ground and greenness, damp with dew, gave everything a glimmering lushness. The dark lake water was calm and as smooth as glass. Amber saw peace and calm she didn't feel.

Of course, Amber wanted to look at the file. Of course, Amber wondered what Sam found on Hunter. It had to be damaging information for her to risk their longtime friendship. Amber understood what Sam did was in her best interest, but she couldn't help but react as she had. Hunter was her husband, the man she loved. They'd built a life together, a place that meant home, a family.

Hunter had his flaws, but who didn't?

Amber herself had committed a terrible crime against Madison and kept it from Hunter, from everyone, all these years. As recently as weeks ago, Amber allowed Madison into their home and family to protect that secret and kept the truth from Hunter.

Secrets are the universal survival language, and Amber's bordered on the criminal.

As despicable and fundamentally deceitful as Amber's actions were, she'd done it for Hunter. She couldn't lose him and would have, had she not done what she did.

What Amber did was for Hunter. Everything Amber did was for Hunter.

Feeling the cause of the rift between the friends was her fault, Madison said, "You don't mean that, Amber. Sam's been your best friend since forever." There was soft sympathy and guilt in her tone.

Amber breathed in and let her breath out sharply. "I want her out of here and out of my life."

Madison stared at Amber's mutinous face. "Sam's not going anywhere. Lily loves her, and she loves Lily."

"I do. Please don't keep me away from Lily or you. You are my best friend, Amber, and I love you." Sam's imploring tone was one Amber hadn't ever heard before.

"You're going to look at the report in this file, or I'll tell Sam everything. I'm the client, and Sam's my lawyer," Madison told Amber.

Amber stiffened, and her throat tightened. "You're the client? Why? Why would you retain her as your lawyer?"

"To help me dig this up." Madison reached for the folder on the table and waved it at Amber. "So, sit down and look at what Sam uncovered for me. Now, Amber." Madison pressed when Amber didn't move.

Amber walked to the table only because she thought her weakened legs wouldn't hold her up. Bracing herself, Amber slid into a chair and reached for the folder. For a long silent moment, she stared at it.

"I know this is difficult, but you need to see this." Madison was eye-to-eye with Amber.

"I don't want to read anymore." Amber's eyes welled up in tears and began to streak down her face, washing the makeup away. The bruise on her cheek had now turned black and blue.

"Oh, Christ." Sam pressed her hand to her mouth. "That sonofabitch did that?"

Madison exchanged a subtle look with Sam to silence her. "Amber, read the entire report."

Sucking in a breath, Amber flipped the manila folder open again. The tension buzzed in her stomach while her eyes scanned the second and third pages of the report. Her stomach tightened, and nausea rose so fast it stole her breath. Amber flipped through the attached deed and bank account statement. The gnawing resentment churning in her pressed down on her chest.

Amber's face devoid of colour, she murmured, "Jesus."

"I'm sorry, Amber," Sam said.

. Amber pushed the papers off the table. "No. No, this isn't Hunter. This is not who he is." Tears blurred her vision.

"I'm sorry, Amber, facts are facts. That's his savings account, a registered company, and downtown apartment." Sam placed her hand lightly on top of Amber's, but she pulled back.

Amber's watery eyes narrowed to thin slits. "Why are you doing this to me?"

"This is the last thing I want you to see, but it's what you need to know," Sam said.

Amber laughed scornfully. "You're enjoying this."

Sam shook her head. "I'm not, Amber."

"Then why show me all of this?" The pain pressing down hard on her chest made it hard for her to breathe.

"Take a deep breath, Amber, and exhale. Madison, get her a glass of water, please."

"I told her to, Amber." Madison ran the tap water and filled the glass. "Because one, you need to know what a waste of sperm Hunter is. Two, you're taking all this back for Lily. And three, we're taking that useless son of a bitch down."

Amber pushed the glass Madison set on the table away. "What if I don't want to?" Amber's mouth was clamped in a thin line.

"You don't have much choice, Amber. I tell Sam everything if you don't, and she'll have no choice but to take you down. She might side with you and release me as a client, but dozens more lawyers are ready and willing to take her place."

Amber closed her eyes and failed to see the concerned look on Sam's face as she wondered what her friend had done to Madison to elicit such anger.

"Stop feeling sorry for yourself, Amber. Sun's coming through dark clouds, and Lily needs to do more than watch television." Madison cleared the table. "We're going to have a tea party, then a B.B.Q., and then we're taking Lily swimming. In between, I'll explain how we will take Hunter down to both of you." Amber dropped her head into crossed arms. "I need to get to work."

The feelings of despair, rejection, and being used as a pawn for financial gains by the man Amber loved cut deep to the bone.

You didn't expect much from people. Years of listening to people on her show blueprint their betrayals taught Amber that. But you expected to trust, to feel loved and safe with family. All Amber felt from Hunter was disappointment, hurt, and pain.

Nothing would be right again.

Chapter 26

THE BRIGHT SUNLIGHT in Madison's eyes had her reaching for the glasses nested in her hair to slip them on. Through yellow-tinted lenses, Madison saw the dew that skimmed over the grass. A summer wind rustled through the leaves wet with rain. Birds flitted through the air, and bees buzzed through the garden delighting in its nectar. Lily was in the pool with Sam while Bessie scurried around its edge, barking and contemplating jumping in.

"Lily's having a great time. She's very much like me and loves to be in the water." Madison watched Sam teaching Lily the backstroke.

In the white, zebra print Swimsuit Madison dug out for Sam from Amber's closet, she looked dramatic and stunning.

"Stop sulking, Amber." Madison turned the grill on to heat. "You weren't any fun at the tea party, and now you're bringing the B.B.Q. mood down."

Splayed on the chaise lounge in shorts and a T-shirt, Amber shifted the wide soft-brimmed hat over her face. Madison forced Amber to join them on the patio, but that didn't mean she had to talk to her.

"Try to smile a little for Lily, Amber. She's having such a good time." Madison closed the lid on the B.B.Q.

Amber pushed herself to a sitting position on the chair and fumbled out a cigarette from the pack on the table.

Connecting lighter to cigarette, she drew in smoke and expelled it in a thin white cloud.

"You really shouldn't do that around Lily."

Amber frowned. "You enjoy controlling people. One, she's nowhere near me. Two, we're in the open, and you may be my puppet master, but not here, not now." Deliberately, Amber blew out a stream of smoke in Madison's direction.

"Mommy, look, I'm swimming." Lily laughed as she kicked water while buoyed by a pink pool noodle.

Amber affixed a smile on her face. "You're doing great, baby."

"Would you like a hamburger or a hot dog?" Madison held up a pack of each.

With a disdainful lift of the brow, Amber said, "Neither, thank you. I'm not hungry."

"Hamburger, it is for you." Madison tossed three hamburger patties on the grill along with the hot dogs. "You'll be hungry when we sit down for lunch." Madison set dishes and cutlery for four on the table.

"Don't pretend we're friends or that you haven't turned my life upside down."

"I didn't, Amber. You and Hunter did that without my help." Madison added the dressing to the garden salad in the wooden bowl and tossed it as Bessie walked up the steps onto the patio and plopped herself next to the B.B.Q. "I had no hand in making what I brought to your attention. I was merely the messenger. I don't understand you. How could you not want to know your husband has been stealing bundles of money from you all this time?"

Amber brought up her knees and circled them with her arms. Her gaze focused on some distant point.

Madison cut a hot dog and tossed half to Bessie, who caught it midair. "Do you know the thought process, planning, and time it took to set his scheme in motion? The balls it took to set up a numbered company to issue invoices from said company for non-rendered services or unsold goods funnel the money to a hidden account and do it for years. The fact he's gone through such elaborate measures to do it calls for anger toward him, not Sam or me."

Sighing a mouthful of smoke, Amber stubbed the cigarette on the ashtray.

"His entitlement is immeasurable. We're talking seven digits of your hard-earned money he stole right from under you." Madison tossed the other half of the hot dog to Bessie, who looked up at her with pleading eyes. "Add the condo Hunter put under his name only." Madison stretched out the last word for emphasis. "It's safe to assume Hunter bought it with your money because you know he doesn't have a pot to piss in."

"It's our money. Not yours, not Sam's, mine and my husband's to do as we want." Amber responded in defence and defiance.

"Yes, it is, but if it's an zzzours, why didn't you know about any of it?" Madison folded the white linen napkins and placed them on each plate.

Amber dropped her gaze and pressed her face to the folded arms on her knees. Christ, she hated Madison.

"I know this must hurt, Amber, and I am sorry for that."

Amber's head whipped up. "Are you? Are you really sorry? You've destroyed my life, my entire existence."

"No, I haven't, Amber." Madison checked on the hamburgers and hot dogs on the grill. They needed another twelve minutes.

"How could you say that?" The tears on Amber's cheeks ran down the colourful bruise, now fully exposed.

"You're your own person, Amber. Everything you are, you've accomplished, not Hunter." Madison looked down at Bessie, tongue lolling, with a smile to win Madison over. She did. "This is the last piece." She tossed the hot dog at Bessie.

"I don't know much about show business, but from what I've read, it sounds cutthroat, a make-it-or-break-it situation. You survived it and advanced in your field. You rose to become the face of the top talk show in the country. I'm not a fan of the bullshit you peddle, and I don't think you are either, but many people are fans, and that's on you, Amber. You did that. Not Hunter."

Amber's eyes filled up. No one had said anything that encouraging or supportive in a long time. "Why are you being so...?"

"Nice?" Madison finished when Amber couldn't bring herself to say it. Madison lowered the B.B.Q. lid to allow the meat to cook faster and took the chair beside Amber. "I was here to destroy you and Hunter. I turned all the money I earned from my shitty, hourly jobs to pay a private detective to get what he could on you and Hunter after I found the two hundred thousand dollar payment to my mother's account."

Amber's eyes cut away from Madison's.

"Yes, Amber, I know about the money you paid my mother. It took me some time to put it together, but I did, and I know everything." Madison gave Amber a twisted grin.

Confusion creased Amber's face. "Yes, of course, but I didn't give your mother two hundred thousand dollars."

"Yes, I know. I'll get to that later. This intricate puzzle has a few pieces, and it took me some time to put it together. Anyway, as I said, my goal was to destroy you along with Hunter until I realized you're as much a victim as I am."

Stung and furious, Amber shouted, "I'm not a victim."

"Keep your voice down." Madison looked over at Lily. Satisfied, Lily's splashing arms had masked Amber's outburst, Madison's eyes cut away from the pool to Amber. "You're very much a victim, Amber. Hunter has groomed you into one. It's what an abuser does. And that's what he is, Amber, an abuser—amongst other things."

The moment's reality and the words' validity hit home and filled Amber with quiet desperation. "I love him."

"I know, but your loving, devoted relationship with Hunter is one-sided. It will always be like trying to grab smoke, it's there, but you're unable to seize it."

Big silent tears coursed down Amber's face. "He completes me."

A sea of denial, Madison thought. "How could he possibly, Amber?"

"As I told you, it's complicated."

"It is, Amber, but not in the way you think."

"What's that supposed to mean?" The anger had faded from her voice.

"You'll see what I mean when I show you the last piece of the puzzle and how the additional one hundred thousand found its way into my mother's account."

"Did you watch me? I swamed alone." Dripping wet, Lily ran up to them excitedly. "I floated on my back and swamed alone."

"We saw you swimming all by yourself, peanut." Madison wrapped Lily in the Big Bird towel. "Soon, you'll become as good a swimmer as a fish."

Lily's eyes popped wide. "You think so, Madison? You really, really think so?"

Madison nodded, and Amber added, "You'll be swimming just like Dory, baby."

Lily's eyes widened. "Woah, like Dory," she whispered reverently and jumped up and down excitedly. That set Bessie into a barking frenzy.

Wrapped in a white sarong, Sam took Lily's hand and reached for Amber to pull her up to join the circle they formed around, yapping Bessie. Madison fell into the ring last between Lily and Sam and thought this was family.

Chapter 27

TOO MUCH SWIMMING, too many hot dogs and ice cream and exhausted, Lily and Bessie napped in her bedroom. Amber, Sam, and Madison gathered in the office.

Madison poured three glasses of cognac. "Drink it, Amber. You'll need it before I show you the last piece of the puzzle."

Amber took the offered glass and braced for the worst, which she sensed, was what was coming. Although how much worse could it get than what she had seen?

How could Hunter do this to her?

Amber had been a devoted, loving wife. She'd kept his home and met his sexual needs, fantasies, and desires. Amber made his longtime dream of owning a restaurant a reality.

Amber would never tell Sam or Madison, but every dime that went into building Hunter's dream came from her. Over the years, it cost her millions to support his vision, but Amber had willingly done it for Hunter.

When Hunter wanted a child, even after her difficulties, she gave him one.

Amber did everything for Hunter, and he stole her dignity and trust, a part of her she'd never get back. Amber felt used and betrayed, hurt, but if he asked her forgiveness, she'd give it to him in a heartbeat.

Hunter completed her.

"Before I show you both this…." Madison picked up her glass and drained it to get the liquid courage she needed. "This is harder than I thought it would be."

"Why does that sound like the lead into something unpleasant?" Amber reached for the cognac bottle and refreshed her drink.

"I'm only showing you this because I need your help. I can't do this on my own. I don't have the legal knowledge you have," Madison looked at Sam, "or the financial resources to do what I need to do." Now she looked at Amber.

Understanding, as much as a fondness she had developed for the scared girl she saw before her, had Sam saying, "We're here for you. Amber and I will help you in any way we can. Won't we, Amber?"

"This is more Hunter bashing, so it's a hard no from me." Amber started to push herself off the sofa.

Madison's eyes held Amber intently, and she sat back down. "Here it goes." Madison inserted the CD and pressed the play button on the laptop.

A breathless hush fell over the room as Sam and Amber watched the video play out.

The dark bedroom was under the soft glow of candles, and their flames burned straight and yellow. An empty bottle of champagne sat next to two half-empty flutes on the dresser. Soft music played in the background, and Amber recognized it as Sade's Sweetest Taboo. A shudder snaked down Amber's spine, and she let out a low gasp, soft enough not to trigger a reaction from either woman.

Although you could only see part of her face, the naked girl lying on the king-size bed was a young Madison—fifteen, sixteen—while the naked man on top of her grunted as he slid in and out of her. His back was to the camera, and they couldn't make out the man's face.

In contrast, with the man who appeared to revel, thrusting himself hard and deep, the look on Madison's face was detached and distant. The act went on for several minutes.

His groan was a feral cry when his body erupted in climax. Before the man rolled off Madison and onto his back, Amber knew who he was. Sade's breathy vocals flowing over the speaker and grunting were too familiar. The man was Hunter.

Amber drank half the cognac in a single pull to wash the shock out of her system. It didn't do the job, and she took the rest of her drink in one gulp.

With a jolt, Sam sat up in her chair. "Jesus Christ."

Madison paused the video. "I was sixteen and a virgin. He was twenty-eight. He was my employer. I'm certain he drugged me that night."

Amber's clamped a hand on her mouth. "Oh, Jesus."

"He got me pregnant," Madison added.

Amber felt her lungs choke up and cut off her breath. She felt faint. Amber breathed in several times, letting the breath out sharply each time. Then the tears formed in Amber's eyes.

"That sonofabitch." Sam bolted to Amber's side. "Oh, Amber, honey, are you all right?"

Amber looked up with eyes shimmering with tears and said, "I don't know what I am," with a wounded look that went deep.

Madison topped Amber's glass and got a refill for herself. "He asked, begged me to get an abortion, and I told him I would." Madison drank. "But I didn't."

"Oh, Jesus Christ." Amber's tears came in sobs now. She hugged her back and rocked back and forth against the consuming pain and guilt. What had she done?

Feeling helpless, Sam did the only thing she could. She gathered her friend in, stroked and soothed her while she cried her pain away. "Let it all out, honey. All of it."

Madison silently watched on.

Sam brushed back the hair that curtained Amber's face. "Do you feel better?"

"I'm never going to feel better." Shoulders hunched, Amber rocked like a child.

"You will, honey. It'll take time, but you will," Sam assured.

"This will stay with me forever."

After a smothering silence, Sam said, "Where's your child, Madison?"

Madison looked Sam in the eyes. "She's upstairs sleeping."

Sam heard incredible words, disjointed words, and nothing made sense. The truth kept turning to confusion the more Madison spoke. "What are you saying?"

"What I'm saying is that Lily's my daughter."

Sam turned to Amber. "What is she talking about?" Amber's blank facial stare that stayed on Sam answered the question. "Jesus Christ! She, not you, is Lily's biological mother." Amber said nothing. "But how?" Shakily, Sam got to her feet and paced the room. "I watched you swell month after month. I visited you in the hospital and saw you hold Lily in your arms hours after her birth."

"Sam. Sam," Madison repeated to stop Sam from stalking the office.

Sam fell back onto the sofa; her limp body inelegantly slumped like an old cushion. "I thought I'd heard every fantastical story from my clients, but to hear it from people dear and near to me is too surreal."

"Listen to me, Sam." Madison snapped her fingers in Sam's face to get her attention. "Sam, pay attention."

"This is a giant clusterfuck." Sam rubbed at her temple at the dull throb on its way to becoming a pressure headache that felt like a drill penetrating her skull.

"It is, but you can put it right for Amber and me." The cognac bottle was empty, and Madison handed Sam a shot of whisky. Sam drank it in one gulp. "I'm going to put out to you the plan I devised. You tell me if it's doable."

"Yeah, whatever." Sam held the empty whiskey glass out for a refill.

"I want Hunter stripped of every penny." Madison poured whisky. "Going the rape route is not an option to destroy him as badly as I want to. Amber can. Amber's legally Lily's mother and Hunter's wife. That being the case, she can fight Hunter for the hidden money, the condominium, and the restaurant." Madison handed Sam the refilled glass. "For Lily."

Sam gave Madison a half brow. "For Lily?"

"Yes, it's for Lily's future. He owes it to her. So tell me, Sam. Is it possible to strip Hunter of his hoard of cash, of everything he owns?" Madison said in a mild tone that was in direct contrast to the fire in his eyes.

"Sure it is, and for Lily, you know I'll go hard, so hard it'll break him. If you don't want to charge him with rape, which you legally could since although you were sixteen, the legal sexual consent age in this country, as your employer, he violated the code."

"I think we can do more damage with Amber going after him. You're not only going to strip him of everything near and dear to him, but I want you to get Amber full custody of Lily. I don't want him anywhere near her."

"I'll do my damnedest, but if she's his daughter...."

"She is his daughter," Madison asserted.

"Okay, then." It made Sam's heart hurt to ask the next question. "Lily's not your biological daughter, Amber. I only need a yes or no answer."

Sam and Madison waited for Amber's response. Amber was pale and looked to be in dark despair. Tears poured from her red-rimmed eyes.

Amber shook her head at Sam.

"Jesus fucking Christ." Sam paused to catch her breath. "That information doesn't leave this room, no way, no how, if I'm going to get anywhere. Understood?"

Madison and Amber nodded.

"To proceed, Amber must petition for a divorce," Sam said.

"So what is it, Amber, divorce or worse?" Madison asked when Amber remained silent.

Amber clutched at her stomach and rocked.

Sam straightened in her seat. "Wait, are you blackmailing Amber?"

"I am," Madison admitted.

"Wow! Shit!" Sam threw back her head and thought for a moment. "As much as I want to know what the hell is going on between you two, I think it best I remain ignorant of this shit show. Christ! How did I not see any of this?" Wearily, Sam brushed a hand through her hair. "I'm going to ask one question. Is it more beneficial if I don't know?"

Madison nodded.

Grudgingly, Sam said, "Okay." Sometimes she hated her job. "What do you say, Amber? Do we start divorce proceedings or not?"

Amber shut her eyes for a moment. "I've loved him absolutely and completely, without reservation."

Sam's mouth opened and closed, deciding it best Amber get her tangles of emotions out of her system.

"I did everything he wanted, gave him everything he wanted, and this is how he repays me?" Amber's soft cries broke Sam's heart.

"I know. I'm sorry, honey."

"You know they say the wife always knows." Amber wiped her cheeks dry. "I knew. I didn't know he was involved with young girls or…. I had no idea about you, Madison. I suspected something, but I never imagined all this other stuff you showed me today."

Madison debated for a moment. "Would you like to know everything, Amber?"

Eyes glazed in disbelief. Amber stared at Madison. "There's more?"

Chapter 28

MADISON ASKED, "ARE you sure you want to know what the more is, Amber?"

"No, I'm not sure of anything anymore, but it can't get worse, can it?" Madison's frowning expression told Amber differently. "Are you serious? The more is worse."

Madison nodded. "Much worse. You can leave the room while I tell Sam if you like. She must have all the information to put on a winnable case." Madison and Sam watched as Amber ran anxious hands over her face.

Amber felt sick all over again. After a long pause, she slid a glance at Madison. "I need to know all of it."

"All right, I'll be right back." Madison returned with a handful of CDs. "I found them in Hunter's apartment together with mine. The others are additional recordings of Hunter with other women at his apartment."

The distress born out of anger, humiliation, and disgust flew into Amber's eyes while Sam's expression remained indifferent. Sam had always suspected Hunter's infidelity, but she saw no proof in the years of marriage to Amber. Sam's suspicion was amplified when Hunter volunteered to help her clean up after the baby shower she threw for Amber and proved what he had in mind was anything but cleaning.

Sam made it clear to Hunter that nothing would happen between them, not then, not ever, and if he tried again, she'd tell Amber everything. Now, Sam realized she shouldn't have turned Hunter away.

Sam assumed Hunter made a move on her to draw a rift between Amber and her, hoping Amber sent her packing. In retrospect, Sam was far off the mark. She should have told Amber the truth and not put hurting her above telling her the truth.

"I watched a few recordings to make sure they were what I suspected. They were, and I couldn't bring myself to watch anymore." Madison turned over the stack of CDs to Sam. "He's been recording his ... encounters, I suspect mainly with young women who work for him at the restaurant, and keeping them as trophies. You may want to watch the rest and decide how to proceed. I thought you could use them as leverage if Hunter refuses to meet our demands."

A terrible feeling of hollowness and guilt settled inside Amber.

"I'll have Lisa, my investigator, and my paralegals review the content and determine how we can apply it to the case," Sam said.

The words filled Amber with genuine regret.

"Do I want to know how you got these?" Sam asked.

Madison overlooked the question. "All you need to know for now is that," Madison looked at Amber and hesitated momentarily, "there are many more at his apartment, in his bedroom closet, above the shelf, behind a fake door."

Sam's eyes widened at Madison's comment. "Jesus."

"I'm sorry, Amber." Madison watched Amber reach for the cigarette pack, and Madison picked up the lighter and fired it up. "Hunter invited me to his apartment for a night together. That's what you saw us talking about by the pool."

Amber's eyes burned fierce and furious. As much as Amber knew the burn she felt wasn't because of what Madison did but because of Hunter, she shouted, "You could have said no."

"I couldn't turn him down. I had to search his apartment for the recording I knew he had. I guessed he would stash it somewhere familiar, somewhere close to him."

Amber didn't take long to put it together, and she stopped her cigarette mid-way to her lips. "That's why you sent the text message." Her voice was unsteady.

Madison nodded. "I hadn't accounted for you to feed Lily too many sugary treats earlier in the day and panic over something so innocuous. The entire scenario played right into my plan, and I used it. I texted Hunter from your cell phone, hoping he'd do the right thing and I could remain in the apartment alone. To my surprise, Hunter did and never suspected a thing. He's not as smart as he thinks he is."

Amber felt a moment's shock, then a surge of anger. Hunter was seducing women in her home, under her nose. She sucked hard on the cigarette.

"I needed the time to go through his apartment." Madison shifted her eyes to Sam. "Hunter called to tell me he couldn't make it and that I should make myself at home. He left a key for me and told me to go for a swim and enjoy the whirlpool. So, in essence, he invited me into his home, and during my visit, I just so happened to wander through his apartment."

"In his bedroom closet, behind a fake door, above the shelf is not necessarily a legal search," Sam pointed out and considered. "I'll make it work."

"I'm sorry you have to hear all this, Amber, but you need to know the truth about the man Hunter is." Madison pushed the ashtray closer to Amber.

"Let's not share this information with anyone," Sam said.

Amber's eyes swam with grief. So many emotions, embarrassment, anger, resentment, hurt, and rejection, were jockeying for position in her. How did a woman survive such infidelity and duplicity perpetrated by the man she loved? Christ, how could she not have known the extent of his deceit?

Any interest in Amber salvaging her marriage was gone now.

Hunter obliterated ten years of marriage, punctured a hole in Amber's heart that would never heal, and shattered her confidence. Hunter single-handedly destroyed her career. The media would have a field day once the news got out. Her career would take a nosedive, and Amber would become persona non-grata.

Amber's world was shrinking.

No one would want to associate themselves with a woman whose husband was a sexual predator. Sexual predator. The words left a sick, vile taste in her throat. How did she wash that away?

They turned at the sound of the barking dog at the door to see a bleary-eyed Lily. The three women pasted a smile on their faces.

Amber and Sam stared at Lily. Both saw so clearly what they hadn't before now. They saw the face so much like Madison's.

"I think I'm hungry. Bessie too." Lily wiped sleep out of her eyes while Bessie scampered around the room.

"Would you like a sliced apple?" Madison offered.

"Okay. Can Bessie have one too?"

"We'll find something for Bessie. Let's go to the kitchen. You too, Bessie, come along."

Amber and Sam watched Madison reach for Lily's hand and walk away. Both bit back the pain of loss at the idea they might never see Lily again.

Epilogue

SUMMER CAME AND went, as did fall, and the winter cold was now in the air. Outside, snow fell thick. The streetlights had gone on, and the snow blanketing the city sparkled white in their gleam.

The house smelled of turkey and ham baking in the oven. Garland hung from staircase railings and door frames. The branches of the seven-foot pine tree in the living room were covered in ornaments, and lights blinked on and off. At its crown hung the star with pink sparkles Lily made in school. Beneath the tree, presents wrapped in shiny red and green paper topped with white bows were stacked high. A maple wood fire burned in the fireplace with a shower of sparks.

It was Madison's first Christmas with Lily, and she was determined to make it memorable.

The recovered videos from Hunter's apartment were incontrovertible evidence he was a predator and a sexual abuser, and he had no option but to plead guilty. Sam and Madison wanted to see Hunter imprisoned for life, but they settled for the twenty-five years imposed to save the women he abused through the trauma of testifying.

Madison stopped taking her mother's calls altogether, which became excessive when the news of Hunter broke. Lacy's calls to Madison weren't made out of concern for her daughter but for gain. News reports estimated five-year-old Lily had come into a five-million-dollar bonanza that included real estate and a five-star restaurant. By Lacy's logic, as Lily's grandmother, she deserved a piece of the pie Samantha Hallstead skillfully secured from the horde of cash and property she seized from Hunter.

To stop Lacy's harassment and demands, Madison had Sam serve Lacy with a protective order and the threat to expose how she attained the two hundred thousand dollars. Only then did Lacy stop calling Madison.

Maybe someday, Madison might forgive her mother for what she had done and reach out to her. That was far into the future because Madison's hurt was too raw.

"Eggnog with a lot of rum to kill the taste of the eggnog." Madison handed the glass to Amber, sitting on the sofa watching Lily show Bessie the ornaments on the tree and the dog barking with delight.

"Thank you. What time is it?" Amber wore a festive red dress with a green cashmere sweater and belt to match. Her wedding finger was naked, but she wore diamonds at her ears and neck. A deserved Christmas present to herself after everything she went through in the past months.

Amber hated that there was still love in her for Hunter. Her therapist told Amber it was normal to feel as she did. Although Hunter betrayed her beyond forgiveness, he had been a part of her life for too long to erase him from her mind overnight. Amber needed time to contend with the emotional and mental turmoil he had left behind.

Dr. McNally was right. With Hunter gone from Amber's life, her feelings for him faded daily, and she was slowly erasing him from her thoughts and her life.

Lily still asked for Daddy, but that was gradually diminishing. Amber told her Daddy went on a long trip and wouldn't return soon. Amber hoped Lily would understand when the time came to tell her the truth. Amber hoped Lily would understand that Hunter gave her full custody and chose to be out of her life for her own good.

Deciding Lily had had enough upheaval with Hunter disappearing from her life, Madison held off telling her she was her mother. Madison decided she and Amber would tell Lily together when the time was right.

"It's nearly six. Christmas Eve dinner will be served as soon as Sam gets here, which I hope is soon. I made a cobb salad, my dressing, of course. There will be sautéed Brussels sprouts with pancetta, homemade gravy and cranberry sauce. For dessert, I made tiramisu, and it all needs to be served soon."

"The culinary classes are paying off." Amber tucked her spread-out legs on the sofa, one under the other to give Madison room to sit.

"I have to improve my cooking for when I take the restaurant over in a few months once the renovations are complete." Erasing Hunter from every aspect of their life was a priority, no matter the cost. "What do you think about renaming the restaurant La Trattoria?"

"It's your restaurant; you can name it what you like."

"It's Lily's restaurant, and your money invested in renovating it. We're partners. The three amigas." Madison smiled when Amber sipped at her eggnog and winced. "It is an acquired taste, but it's Christmas, and I never did the Christmassy thing. So, we're doing everything Christmas. You promised." Madison raised her eggnog glass in a toast.

"I did." Amber sipped more eggnog and put on an overstated smile on her face.

"Bessie wants to open this present." From under the tree, Lily picked up the box closest to her. Her large, round eyes glowed with delight, and her curly hair tumbled around it. She wore a red dress with elves stamped and a white collar.

"Bessie's going to have to wait until tomorrow morning. Christmas Day is when presents are opened," Madison said.

"But she really, really, really wants to open it." Lily pushed her lower lip beyond her upper to win Madison and Amber over.

Madison reached for her cell phone on the table. "Let me see where Santa's at and ask if he'll allow Lily and Bessie to open the present and risk losing all the other presents because they're impatient."

Lily set the present back under the tree. "That's okay. Bessie and I will wait until tomorrow. Auntie Sam still has to put her presents under the tree."

"She does, and that's a great idea. Why don't you and Bessie go to the office and watch Frosty The Snowman? It's on channel six," Madison said.

"Okay. Come on, Bessie. We're going to watch television."

When Lily left the room, Amber studied Madison over the rim of her glass. "Why didn't you tell Sam what I did?"

Madison rose from the sofa, walked to the fireplace, and tossed a log into the fire. "I planned to tell Sam everything. When I learned your best friend was a criminal lawyer, I planned to have her represent me and turn her against you. I hoped to hurt you as much as you hurt me in many ways, and Telling Sam you paid my mother one hundred thousand dollars to switch your stillborn baby for my healthy girl would have put a deep nail in your coffin as I wanted to."

Amber watched Madison move the log into place with the poker sending embers rising into the chimney. "Why didn't you?"

"After I moved in here, I began to see things and realized you were as much a victim of Hunter's as I was. Fear and dependence are how abusers control women, and as independent as you appeared on the screen, I could see you were deep under the spell of an abuser. I understood his manipulation made you fear losing him if you didn't give him the child he wanted, and what you did, you did because of him."

Nodding, Amber dropped her gaze to the glass of eggnog between her hands. How was it that a girl decades younger saw what she hadn't?

"Over the years, he conditioned you to become so dependent on him you'd do anything he wanted."

Amber nodded again. "My therapist has helped me to see and understand that."

Madison returned the poker to the stand by the fireplace. "What you didn't know is that weeks before you gave birth, my mother met with Hunter to tell him I hadn't aborted the baby as he asked me to do and that he was about to become a father. When Hunter found out, he gave my mother one hundred thousand dollars to get rid of my baby."

"Christ, I didn't know. How do you know all this?"

"A private investigator I hired. It cost me every dime I earned, but he was the best. It took him months of investigation to piece it all together, but the ball got rolling when he found out you and I were both in the hospital, at the same time, giving birth, and my mother was assigned as our nurse."

"That does sound too coincidental."

Nodding, Madison turned to face Amber. "That was my thought, and it triggered stored memories in me to the surface, and her duplicity became apparent. My treacherous, conniving mother was behind, making me think my baby was stillborn."

"What made you suspect Lily wasn't your baby?"

"Things my mother said and a nagging feeling. When I found the money in her account and traced it back to you and Hunter, I had, Hope exhumed for DNA testing, and she matched your DNA, not mine."

Amber felt her stomach lurch. "Jesus. How did you get my DNA?"

"You'd be surprised what you can do when motivated enough. And finding my baby was my motivation."

Amber's shocked eyes stared back while she processed what she was told.

Madison set aside her eggnog and walked to the bar to pour two cognac glasses. "I think this conversation warrants something stronger."

Amber tossed back the drink when Madison handed her the glass. Amber stopped mid-way through her drinking when the thought hit her. "Did Lacy do something to my baby to make the switch happen?" There was a sick ball in the pit of Amber's stomach. "The coroner's report listed the cause of death as stillborn, but Lacy's a nurse and has access to all sorts of drugs. What if she...." Amber couldn't bring herself to say the word murder." Agitated, Amber rose to pace the room. "I need to report this to the police."

"Amber, stop, breathe. That's all conjecture, a theory. Breathe in and exhale. Again." Madison guided Amber's breathing when she stopped pacing. Calmer now, Madison waved Amber to sit on the sofa. "Think about it, Amber. You go to the police, and everything comes out. You were an accomplice and could end up in prison. You could lose everything. You were drowning in a mess Hunter created but surfaced unscathed. Your career and show are thriving because your female audience sympathizes with you. You can't throw that away."

The career Amber carved out was all she had now. Lily was still in her life, but as much as Madison told Amber she would continue to be, there were no guarantees. If Amber learned anything in the past few months, it was that there were no assurances in life.

"I don't care about my career. I need to find out the truth. That Lacy may have caused my child's death will remain in my mind." Amber's breath hitched.

"Relax, Amber. My mother's greedy, not a murderer. She didn't do any of those things."

Amber caught the telltale look in Madison's eyes. "You had the baby tested for drugs."

Madison nodded. "No drugs and no suffocation. Your baby's death was due to natural causes."

Amber threw back her head on the back of the sofa and fell into a reflective silence, and Madison joined her.

"What would you have done if the results came back differently?" Amber said after some time.

The doorbell chimed, and they heard Lily rush to open the front door. "Auntie Sam's here. Mommy, Madison, help me open the door. I can't reach the lock thing." Lily called out as Bessie jumped to help.

"I'm coming, peanut," Madison called out. "We're celebrating Christmas tonight, Amber. So no dark thoughts, agreed?" Madison's eyes remained on Amber until she nodded.

Christmas carols drifted from the dining room speakers. Candles flickered on the table, teeming with a golden turkey, a ham and the delicious side dishes Madison made. There was an uncorked bottle of chilled Beaujolais on the table and another in the refrigerator, waiting to be consumed over great food and wonderful conversation.

During dinner, there was chatter from Lily's excited talk about Santa and Rudolph's imminent visit. As stuffed as Bessie was from the turkey Lily tossed her all through dinner, she managed to zoom around the dining room to match Lily's excitement.

It was the best Christmas. Madison had long forgotten what it was to feel at peace, devoid of hate and anger. Tonight there was only happiness in Madison.

Sneak peek at M.L. Lexi's new novel

THE FEARLESS WOMAN

Prologue

EVERYONE LIVES WITH the unspoken understanding of their obsoleteness. Still, you're never ready when it becomes your reality.

The idea that the inward comfort derived from a job Olivia had devoted twenty-five years of her life could be snatched away overnight made the anger spring hot inside her. Olivia cast enraged blue eyes to the email and reread it. The email from Catherine Sullivan, the president of Sullivan Foods, contained six lines of diplomatically correct legalese and the tenor of a sacking. Six aloof lines on an email were the sum of Olivia's years of commitment and loyalty to Catherine Sullivan.

Olivia's anger hot and pulsing, she bolted from the couch and paced the living room. Oreo, Olivia's black and white Maltese Shih Tzu, followed suit.

"Twenty-five fucking years I gave her. I worked nights and weekends without compensation. I never took a sick day, ever. I gave Catherine all I had, all of me, only to be fired over an email. She didn't even have the guts to say it to my face." Olivia's voice trembled with rage, and she increased her pace. Oreo withdrew to the couch. Comfort over exercise.

Olivia never saw it coming, but she blamed no one but herself for her employer sending her packing after years of loyal service. Deluding herself to believe that devoting her time, effort, heart and soul to her job would lead her employer to recognize her contribution rather than push her out the door was her mistake.

The boomer mentality of loyalty to your employer ingrained from a young age was corporate propaganda from institutions extorting a surplus of people seeking employment. Olivia knew that now, but it was too little too late.

Wisdom came at great cost.

There had been many little warning bells leading to this moment that Olivia chose to overlook for the sake of a much needed paycheque. The first overlooked red flag was when Catherine, the woman she looked up to and respected, knocked Olivia's salary by four thousand dollars. Catherine did so without explanation or cause at a vulnerable time in Olivia's life, knowing Olivia wouldn't contest it.

Olivia's nasty divorce left her in debt and desperate for money, and she couldn't afford to dispute the pay cut.

The second overlooked warning signal was when Catherine failed to pay Olivia the commission she'd worked for months to get. Again, Olivia did nothing. Financial insecurity leads to compliance, and Catherine knew it.

What Catherine did was beyond the pale and fundamentally dishonest. Still, Catherine continued to take advantage of Olivia, and Olivia had no choice but to allow it. Losing her home and not eating wasn't an option.

The hard-learned survival lessons taught Olivia that life was inherently unfair and pride was a commodity when debts were mounting.

Olivia had Bob to thank for the poor state of her finances. After ten years of marriage to Bob Huntley, he walked out on their marriage and left Olivia with more debt than she imagined one person could accrue. Marital debt, they called it, when Bob disappeared into thin air, and Olivia was on the hook for the entire amount. Never mind that Bob had forged her signature on the credit card applications or the second mortgage documents and cleaned out their bank accounts.

It took Olivia years to pay off the debt she was left to shoulder and just as long to gain her financial footing. With the debt paid, the massive boulder on her shoulders slid away. Olivia had never felt as free or as secure as she did then.

Independence accomplished, Olivia shed Bob's surname and reclaimed her maiden name. Falco wasn't regal or a legacy name, but it was hers, and Olivia Huntley became Olivia Falco.

Under the name Olivia Falco, she opened bank and investment accounts. Managing her money, bank accounts, and investments, something Bob didn't allow during their marriage, felt liberating.

Bob had controlled their finances and purposely kept Olivia in the dark during their marriage. It wasn't until Bob left that Olivia discovered he was as bad a money manager as he was a husband. It wasn't until then she went over the credit card statements and saw the gambling charges. It wasn't until then she saw the motel charges and, on deeper detecting, found out he was "entertaining" a parade of women.

Aside from trusting Bob and leaving him in charge of their finances, marrying him was something Olivia would regret all her life.

But there was a silver lining to every dark cloud. Olivia's cheating, lying husband helped her recognize her inner strength and self-reliance. That knowledge gave Olivia control over her life, the money she never had with Bob, and a taste of independence. It tasted great, and keeping her newfound freedom was a powerful motivator for Olivia to do everything necessary to maintain it.

Olivia gave everything she had to her job and the company that helped make it possible to get her life in order. She walked the line and did what was asked of her. She went above and beyond because she was grateful, loved her job and colleagues, and owed Sullivan Foods for where she was today.

That rationale was Olivia's grievous mistake. It was abundantly clear from Catherine's email that Olivia was an employee of Sullivan Foods and nothing more.

The most painful betrayal is always from the people you trust the most.

Broken and exhausted, Olivia curled up on the couch with Oreo and cried.

Coming Soon

The Complete Woman
The Conflicted Woman
The Spiteful Woman
The Tortured Woman

The Relentless Woman Duology

The Relentless Woman
The Vindictive Women

The Unbreakable Woman Trilogy

The Unbreakable Woman
The Brave Woman
The Valiant Woman

Contact us

Email us at mllexiauthor@gmail.com to receive emails whenever M.L. Lexi publishes a new book. There is no charge or obligation and your information will remain confidential.

Visit us at www.mllexi.com to read excerpts of upcoming releases.

www.ingramcontent.com/pod-product-compliance
Lightning Source LLC
Chambersburg PA
CBHW051242170626
46809CB00004B/1435